MW00755761

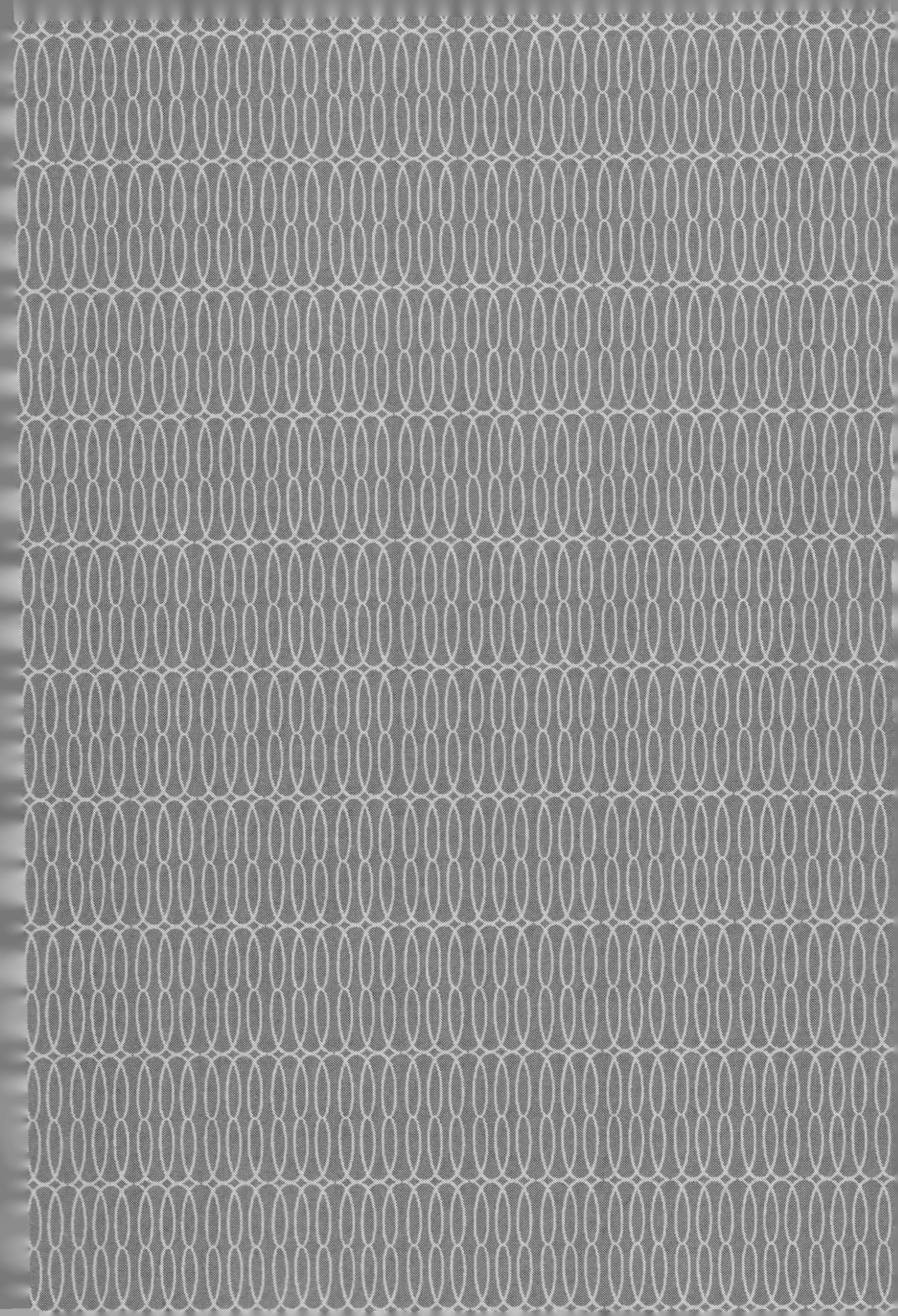

Bonjour Tristesse

Bonjour Tristesse

Françoise Sagan

Translated from the French by Irene Ash

Introduction by Diane Johnson

AN ecco BOOK

HARPERPERENNIAL MODERNCLASSICS

NEW YORK • LONDON • TORONTO • SYDNEY • NEW DELHI • AUCKLAND

HARPERPERENNIAL MODERNCLASSICS

First English edition published by E.P. Dutton & Co. in 1955.

P.S. is a trademark of HarperCollins Publishers.

BONJOUR TRISTESSE. Copyright © 1955 by E.P. Dutton & Co. Inc. Introduction copyright © 2001 by Diane Johnson. All rights reserved. Printed in the United States of America. No part of this book may be used or reproduced in any manner whatsoever without written permission except in the case of brief quotations embodied in critical articles and reviews. For information address HarperCollins Publishers, 10 East 53rd Street, New York, NY 10022.

HarperCollins books may be purchased for educational, business, or sales promotional use. For information please write: Special Markets Department, HarperCollins Publishers, 10 East 53rd Street, New York, NY 10022.

First Ecco paperback edition published 2001.

First Harper Perennial Modern Classics edition published 2008.

Designed by Cassandra J. Pappas

Library of Congress Cataloging-in-Publication Data
has been applied for.

ISBN 978-0-06-144079-3

08 09 10 11 12 DC/RRD 10 9 8 7 6 5 4 3 2 1

Introduction

NEARLY HALF A CENTURY AGO, in 1954, readers in France (and the following year in the United States) were excited by a first novel by the pert, talented teenager Françoise Sagan. France has had its share of spellbinding young prodigies, from Rimbaud to Radiguet. Colette herself was in her twenties with the first of her *Claudine* novels. Sagan, too, was immediately accorded a place in the ranks of very young people who had produced a work precocious in its technical brilliance, and engaging because of the perhaps inadvertent charm of its knowing, world-weary tone. It was not long before Sagan (born Françoise Quoirez in 1935) was perhaps—for American readers, in any case—the most famous of all French writers.

Such stories of discovery are always charming. *Bonjour Tristesse* is a brief, bittersweet tale that recounts a summer in the life of Cécile, a seventeen-year-old who, it appeared, was very much like the author herself, a girl of good family who had written it in the garden of her parent's country house and sent the manuscript to three publishers at once. The man reading it for the publisher René Julliard rushed to the phone and advised Julliard to lose no time in signing up the unknown author. Julliard immediately called her family's apartment in Paris at eleven that morning, only to be told by the maid that "Mademoiselle dort encore" (Mademoiselle is still asleep). Julliard evidently called back.

It was, of course, hard to separate the life and tone of the narrator, Cécile, from those of the author herself. Both were seventeen (Sagan was eighteen when the novel came out), and it was easy to conflate their circumstances. Readers would speculate on how well the author was aware of and understood the emotional situation of her heroine—a girl who adores her father and schemes against his mistresses to keep his love for herself. Is it a skillful fiction or an inadvertent revelation? In the novel the father is a charming rogue, dissolute and promiscuous, and the mother is conveniently dead so that he can have the romantic adventures essential to the plot.

However sophisticated the writer, the narrator is not conscious of revealing what to the reader is classic and clear: a young girl, jealous of her father's relationships with older, sexually experienced women, seeks to destroy them at the same time she herself becomes sexually active. The reader, if not the girl herself, will see that she hopes to provoke her father's jealousy in turn. Are its glamorously amoral triangles somewhat more colorful, people wondered, than the author's actual family situation?

In any case, readers marveled at the elegance and brilliance of someone so young, at her worldly cynicism and sophistication, at the callousness of the young narrator and the decadence of the French social set she depicted. Even more, perhaps, after the recent bleak wartime years, people yearned for its luxury and the self-indulgence it portrays. For Americans in particular, it embodied what readers of the time admired about France, the French ability to freely enact psychic realities—Oedipal, hostile, exotic—that Americans acknowledged but kept sternly in check. It was also a period when French literature was especially admired in America, and was more often translated than is the case today.

It is in the decor of the novel that the reader of today will find a certain period charm, perhaps even feel a nostalgic regret for the innocence of the pleasure people took in the 1950s in pastimes now disapproved of or forbidden. People sunburned with impunity—there was no sunscreen, anyhow—and everyone smoked all the time. It is almost hard to remember now how everyone smoked and drank and drove. From today's perspective, the ending is foreshadowed with a clarity that is almost clumsy: "Anne's car . . . was a huge American convertible, which she kept more for publicity than to suit her own taste, but it suited mine down to the ground, with all its shiny gadgets. . . ." "I dare say I owed most of my pleasures of that period to money; the pleasure of driving fast in a high-powered car. . . ." The mind's eye produces one of those huge gas-guzzling cars with tail fins that would be coffins for fifties icons like James Dean.

Each epoch gets the denouement it deserves, and the car crash was to 1950s fiction denouements what a death by tuberculosis or brain fever had been in earlier eras: the default solution, a poignant resolution that seemed also to correspond to reality (the deaths of James Dean, Albert Camus, Françoise Dorléac, the sister of Catherine Deneuve). Not just a cliché, a car crash was a double-duty device that conveniently eliminated characters the author wished to kill off—for instance as Mary McCarthy did in the end of her novel *A Charmed Life*—while assuming moral dimensions symbolizing mistake or retribution, just as other forms of death, appropriate to other ages, have also done in their day. It is not uninteresting that Sagan would later herself be involved in a serious and debilitating car crash.

How American college students of almost her same age (like this writer) thrilled at Cécile's complete absence of concern for the future and, even more so, at the attitude of the adults in her life, so unlike that of our own parents:

> "How did you make out with your examinations?" "Flunked!" I said, cheerfully. "Completely flunked." "But you must pass in October, you absolutely must!"
>
> "Why should she?" my father interrupted. "I never got any diploma and I manage to live very well. . . . My daughter will always have a man to take care of her. . . ."

A man taking care of us might be the dull fate of all of us, we knew, but Françoise Sagan had avoided it, had written a bestseller, and was even said to have bought a house with her casino winnings.

Cécile, if not Françoise, was inspiringly wild. "Kisses alone can cease to satisfy, and no doubt if Cyril had not been so fond of me, I would have become his mistress that very week," she says with characteristic irony. Among the risky behaviors available, pregnancy, however, was not countenanced, and abortion, then illegal in France, was spoken of in *Bonjour Tristesse* with frankness unusual in novels of the time. Anne, Cécile's father's mistress, warns her of going too far with Cyril: "You should realize that such diversions usually end up in a hospital." This is a warning most women readers of the same age had received, but in that heyday of existential despair, Cécile's indifference to received behavior struck a particularly thrilling note of vicarious danger with square young Americans as well as studious French lycée pupils preparing their baccalaureates.

Everyone praised the young author's ease with narrative. The point of view and the chronology are skillfully managed. The story is told some months after the action, but the narrator gives us, simultaneously, her point of view before she became aware and the point of view of her disillusioned and unhappy present, the self that has said *bonjour* to *tristesse*, unhappiness. At the same time, these limited points of view convey to the reader an understanding the narrator does not herself possess. "An unthinking, easy egoism had been natural to me," she says, implying that she is cured of egotism. But we see she does not really gain understanding;

she has only entered into a new state of self-indulgent resentment and determination. Even at the end, when her efforts to prevent her father's marriage have been all too successful, though she feels remorse she has not really gained mature self-knowledge, only an intimation that the future will not be satisfying. What she believes she knows of herself ("I have always been fickle, and I have no wish to delude myself on this point") is itself a delusion the reader can easily see.

If Cécile does not gain understanding of herself, her clear-sighted, rather cruel diagnosis of French society remains astonishing. Libertines like her father have a certain fate: "A time comes when they are no longer attractive or in good form. They can't drink any more, and they still hanker after women. Only then they have to pay heavily and lower their standards, to escape from their loneliness. Then they are really laughingstocks." And she notes that women like Anne and Elsa have no capital but their beauty and luck, or lack of it, in finding men to keep them.

"In order to achieve inner peace, my father and I had to have excitement," says Cécile. Sagan herself, it is worth noting, must be somewhat the same, in that she has gone on to an immensely productive literary career—nearly thirty novels—at least two of which, *A Certain Smile* (1956) and *Aimez-Vous Brahams* (1959), were well received in the United States—seven plays, memoirs, and journals—which has perhaps been excitement of the right kind.

—Diane Johnson

April 2001

Part One

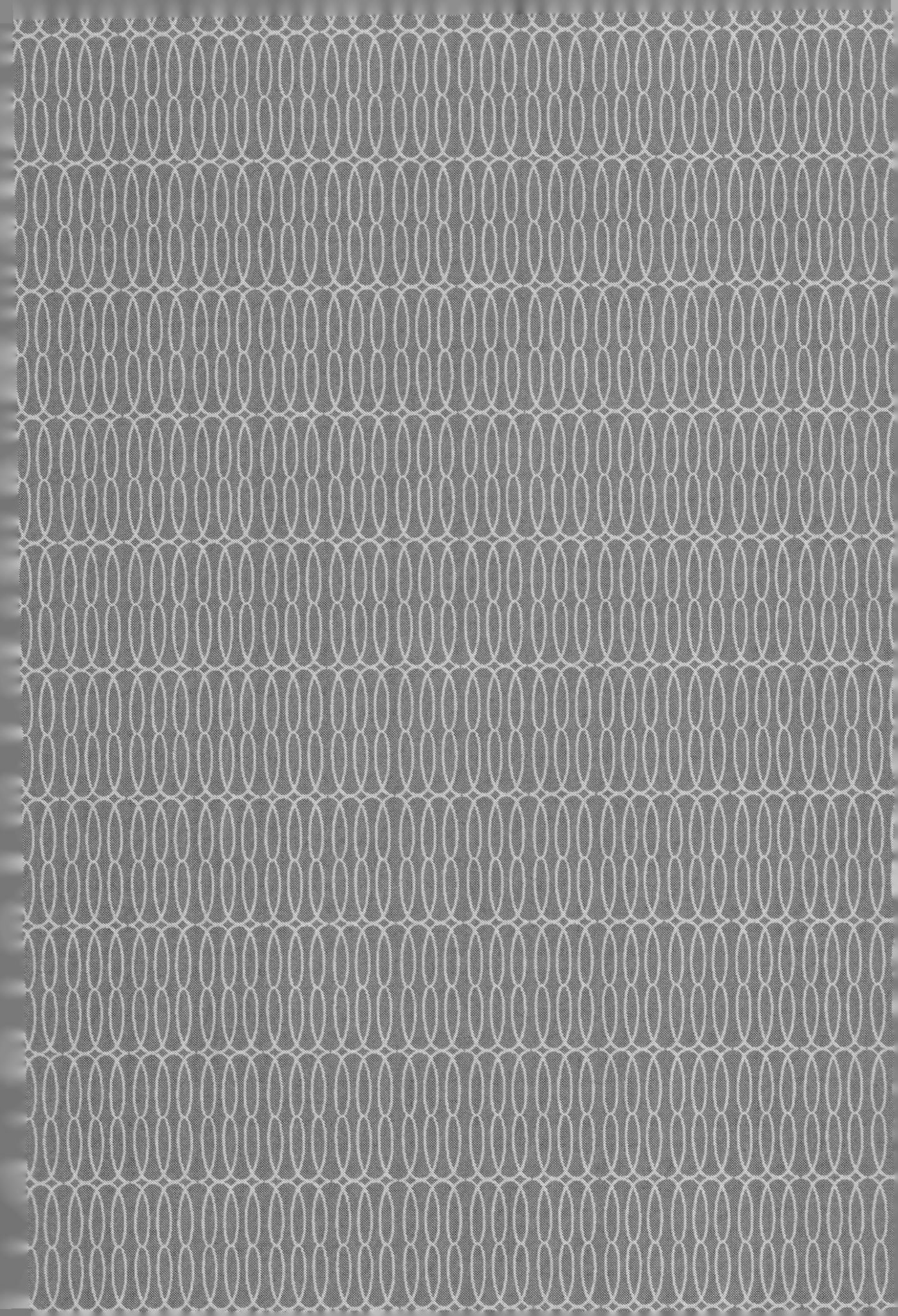

Adieu tristesse
Bonjour tristesse
Tu es inscrite dans les lignes du plafond
Tu es inscrite dans les yeux que j'aime
Tu n'es pas tout à fait la misère
Car les lèvres les plus pauvres te dénoncent
Par un sourire
Bonjour tristesse
Amour des corps aimables
Puissance de l'amour
Dont l'amabilité surgit
Comme un monstre sans corps
Tête désappointée
Tristesse beau visage.

P. ELUARD.
(La vie immédiate.)

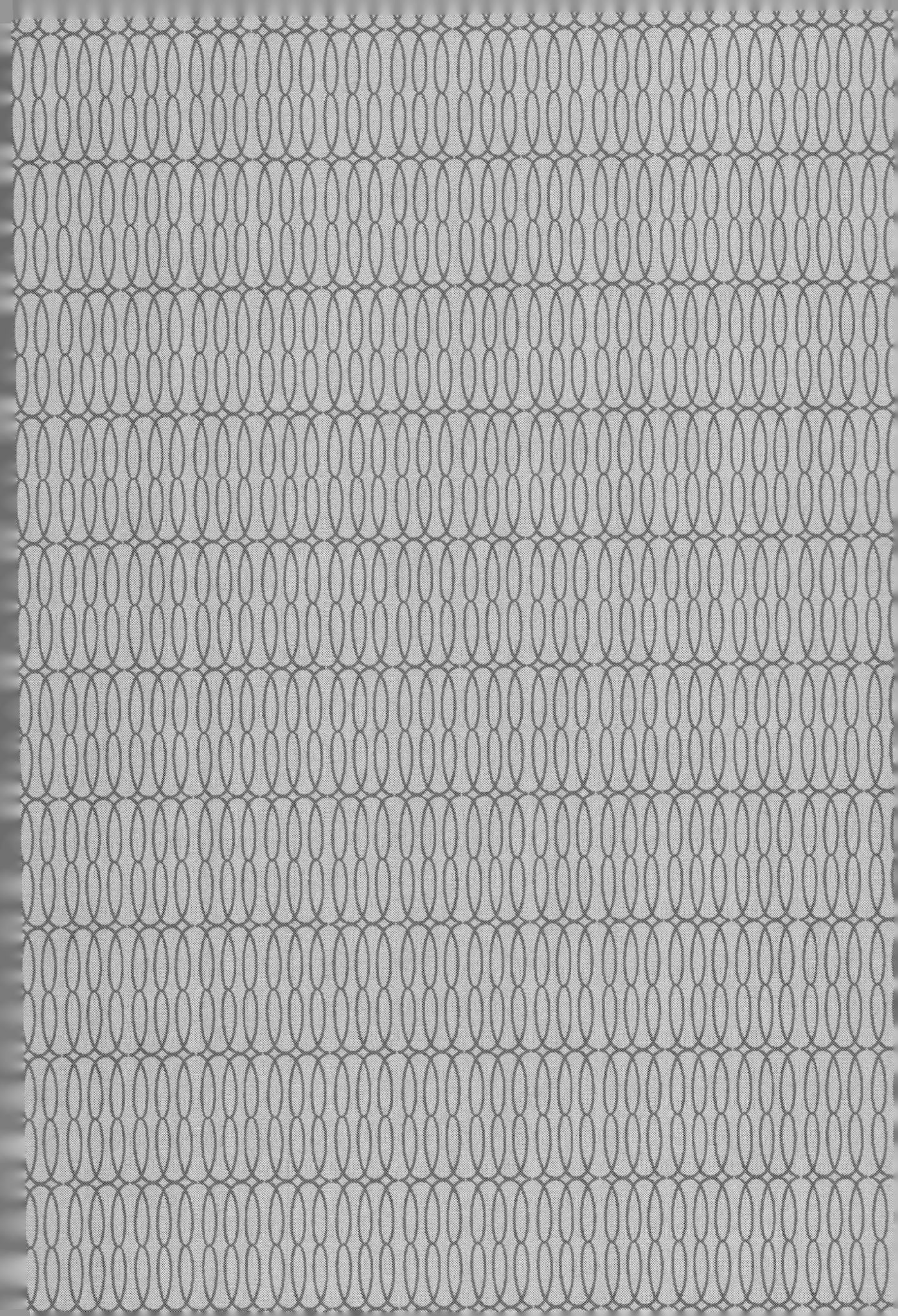

One

A STRANGE MELANCHOLY pervades me to which I hesitate to give the grave and beautiful name of sorrow. The idea of sorrow has always appealed to me, but now I am almost ashamed of its complete egoism. I have known boredom, regret, and occasionally remorse, but never sorrow. Today it envelops me like a silken web, enervating and soft, and sets me apart from everybody else.

THAT SUMMER, I was seventeen and perfectly happy. At that time "everybody else" was my father and his mistress, Elsa. I must explain this situation at once, or it might give a false impression. My father was forty, and had been a widower for fifteen years. He was young for his age, full of vitality and liveliness. When I left my convent school two years before and came to Paris to live with him, I soon realized that he was living with a woman. But I was slower in accepting the fact that his fancy changed every six months! But gradually his charm, my new easy life, and my own disposition, led me to fall in readily with his ways. He was a frivolous man, clever at business, always curious, quickly bored, and very attractive to women. It was easy for me to love him, for he was kind, generous, gay and fond of me. I cannot imagine a better or a more amusing companion. At the beginning of the summer I am concerned with now, he even asked me whether I would object to having Elsa along on our summer vacation. She was his mistress of the moment, a tall, red-headed girl, sensual and worldly, kindly, rather simple-minded, and unpretentious. One might have come across her any day in the studios and bars of the Champs-Elysées. I readily consented, for I knew his need of a woman, and I knew, too, that Elsa would not get in our way. Besides, my father and I were so delighted at the prospect of going away that I was in no mood to object to anything. He had rented a large white villa on the Mediterranean, for which we had been longing since the spring. It was remote and beautiful, standing on a headland jutting over the sea, hidden from the road by pine woods. A goat path led down to a small, sunny cove where the sea lapped against rust-colored rocks.

The first days were dazzling. We spent hours on the

beach giving ourselves up to the hot sun, gradually assuming a healthy golden tan—except for Elsa, whose skin reddened and peeled, causing her intense agony. My father performed all sorts of complicated exercises to reduce a rounding stomach unsuitable for a Don Juan. From dawn onward I was in the water. It was cool and transparent, and I plunged wildly about in my efforts to wash away the shadows and dust of Paris. I lay stretched out on the sand, took up a handful and let it run through my fingers in soft, yellow streams. I told myself that it ran out like time. It was an idle thought, and it was pleasant to have idle thoughts, for it was summer.

On the sixth day I saw Cyril for the first time. He was hugging the coast in a small sailboat and capsized in front of our cove. I had a wonderful time helping him to rescue his things, during which he told me his name, that he was studying law, and was spending his vacation with his mother in a neighboring villa. He had a typically Latin face—very dark and very frank. There was something responsible and protective about him which I liked at once. Usually I avoided college students, whom I considered brutal, wrapped up in themselves, particularly in their youth, in which they found material for drama, or an excuse for their own boredom. I did not care for young people; I much preferred my father's friends, men of forty, who spoke to me courteously and tenderly—treated me with the gentleness of a father—or a lover. But Cyril was different. He was tall and almost beautiful, with the kind of good looks that immediately inspires one with confidence. Although I did not share my father's intense aversion to ugliness—which often led us to associate with stupid people—I did feel vaguely uncomfortable in the presence of anyone completely devoid of physical charm. Their resignation to the fact that they were unattractive seemed to me somehow indecent. For what are we looking for if not to please? I do not know if the desire to attract others comes from a superabundance of vitality, possessiveness, or the hidden, unspoken need to be reassured.

When Cyril left he offered to teach me to sail. I went up to dinner absorbed in my thoughts of him, and hardly spoke during the meal or noticed my father's nervousness. After dinner we stretched out in chairs on the terrace as usual. The sky was studded with stars. I gazed upward, vaguely hoping to see a sudden, exciting flash across the heavens, but it was early in July and too soon for shooting stars. On the terrace the crickets were chirping. There must have been thousands of them, drunk with heat and moonlight, pouring out their song all night long. I had been told they made the sound by rubbing their legs together, but I preferred to believe that it came from the throat, guttural, instinctive like the howls of cats in heat.

We were very comfortable. A few tiny grains of sand between my skin and my shirt kept me from dropping off to sleep. Suddenly my father coughed apologetically and sat up.

"Someone is coming to stay with us," he announced.

I shut my eyes in disappointment. We had been too happy; it just couldn't last!

"Hurry up and tell us who it is!" cried Elsa, always avid for gossip.

"Anne Larsen," said my father, and he turned toward me.

"I asked her to come if she was worn out by the collections and she . . . she's coming."

Anne was the last person I would have thought my father would ask to visit us. She had been a friend of my mother's, and had very little connection with my father. Just the same, when I left the convent school two years before and my father was at his wits' end about me, he had asked her to take me in hand. Within a week she had dressed me in the right clothes and taught me something about life. I remember thinking her the most wonderful person and being quite embarrassingly fond of her. But she soon managed to transfer my affections to a young man she knew. To her I owed my first taste of fashion and my first flirtation, and I was very grateful. At forty-two she was a most attractive woman, much sought after, with a beautiful face, proud, calm, reserved. This aloofness was the only complaint one could make against her. But she was kind as well as aloof. Everything about her denoted a strong will, an inner serenity which was awesome. Although divorced now, she seemed to have no lovers; but then we did not know the same people. Her friends were clever, intelligent and discreet. Ours, from whom my father demanded only good looks or amusement, were loud and insatiable. I think she rather despised us for our love of diversion and frivolity, as she despised all extremes. We had few points of contact except through the world of business and the memory of my mother. Her work was concerned with women's fashions and my father's with publicity, so they met occasionally at professional dinners. Added to this were my own determined efforts to keep in touch with her, because, although she awed me, I greatly admired her. So her unexpected appearance here worried me because of Elsa's presence and Anne's ideas on my upbringing.

Elsa went up to bed after making detailed inquiries about Anne's social position. I remained alone with my father and moved over to the steps, where I sat at his feet. He leaned forward and put his hands on my shoulders.

"Why are you so thin, darling? You look like a little wildcat. I'd like to have a lovely, buxom, fair-haired daughter with china-blue eyes and . . ."

"That's hardly the point," I said. "What made you invite Anne, and why did she accept?"

"Perhaps she wants to see your old father, you never know."

"You're not the type of man to interest Anne," I said.

"She's too intelligent and has too much self-respect. And what about Elsa? Have you thought of her? Can you imagine what Elsa and Anne can talk about? I can't!"

"I'm afraid it hadn't occurred to me," he confessed. "But you're right, it's a dreadful thought. Cécile, my sweet, shall we go right back to Paris?"

He laughed softly and rubbed the back of my neck. I turned to look at him. His dark eyes gleamed; funny little wrinkles marked their edges; his mouth was turned up slightly. He looked like a faun. I laughed with him as I always did when he created complications for himself.

"My little partner in crime," he said. "What would I do without you?"

His voice was so serious yet so tender that I knew he would really have been unhappy without me. Late into the night we talked of love, of its complications. In my father's eyes they were all imaginary. He refused categorically all ideas of fidelity or serious commitments. He explained that they were arbitrary and sterile. From anyone else such views would have shocked me, but I knew that in his case they did not exclude tenderness and devotion—feelings which came all the more easily to him since he was determined that they should be transient. This conception of quick, tempestuous and passing love affairs I found enticing. I was not at the age when fidelity is attractive. And of course, I knew little of love: the meetings, the kisses, the weary aftermath.

Two

ANNE WAS NOT EXPECTED for another week, and I made the most of these last days of real freedom. We had rented the villa for two months, but I knew that once she was there it would be impossible for any of us to relax completely. Anne gave a shape to things and a meaning to words that my father and I preferred to ignore. She set a standard of good taste and fastidiousness which one could not help noticing in her sudden withdrawals, the look on her face, and her hurt silences. It was both stimulating and exhausting, but in the long run humiliating, because I could not help feeling that she was right.

On the day of her arrival we decided that my father and Elsa should meet her at the station in Fréjus. I firmly refused to go with them. In desperation my father cut all the gladioli in the garden to offer her as soon as she got off the train. My only advice to him was not to allow Elsa to carry the bouquet. After they had left I went down to the beach. It was three o'clock and the heat was overpowering. I was lying on the sand half asleep when I heard Cyril calling to me. I opened my eyes; the sky was white, shimmering with heat. I made no reply, because I did not want to speak to him, or to anyone. I was nailed to the sand by all the strength of summer heat—my arms were like lead, my mouth dry.

"Are you dead?" he said. "From over there you looked like something washed up by the sea."

I smiled. He sat down near me and my heart began to beat faster, more heavily, because his hand had just touched my shoulder. A dozen times during the past week my brilliant seamanship had cast us into the water, our arms entwined, and I had not felt the least twinge of excitement. But today the heat, my being half-asleep and his accidental touch had somehow broken down my defenses. I turned my head toward him. I was getting to know him better. He was steady, more strait-laced than is perhaps usual at his age. For this reason my family situation, our unusual domestic trio, shocked him. He was too kind or too timid to tell me, but I felt it in the oblique looks of disapproval he gave my father. It would have pleased him if I had let him know that I, too, was tormented by this situation. But I was not. In fact my only torment at that moment was the way my heart was thumping. He bent over me. I thought of the past few days, of my feeling of peace and confidence when I was with him, and I was tempted to resist the touch of his soft, full lips on mine.

"Cyril," I said. "We were so happy . . ."

But his kiss was gentle. I looked at the sky, then saw nothing but lights bursting under my closed eyelids. The warmth, the dizziness, and the savor of our first kisses went on for a long moment. The sound of a motor horn pulled us apart guiltily. I left Cyril without a word and went up to the house. I was surprised that the car was back so soon; Anne's train could hardly have arrived as yet. But there was Anne on the terrace, just getting out of her own car.

"This is as silent as the house of the Sleeping Beauty," she said. "How brown you are, Cécile! I am so pleased to see you."

"I, too," I answered. "But have you just come from Paris?"

"I decided to drive down. And, by the way, I'm exhausted."

I showed her to her room and opened the window, hoping to catch a glimpse of Cyril's boat. It had disappeared. Anne sat down on the bed. I noticed little shadows around her eyes.

"What a delightful villa!" she said. "Where's the master of the house?"

"He's gone to meet you at the station, with Elsa."

I had put her suitcase on a chair, and when I turned

around I received a shock. Her face had suddenly collapsed; her mouth was trembling.

"Elsa Mackenbourg? He brought Elsa Mackenbourg here?"

I could not think of anything to say. I looked at her, completely stupified. Was this the face I had always seen so calm and controlled? Her eyes were on me, still I realized she saw not me but the images my words had given her. Finally she saw my expression and looked away.

"I ought to have given you a little more time before coming," she said. "But I was in such a hurry to get away and so tired."

"And now . . ." I went on like an automaton.

"Now *what?*" she said.

Her expression was purely an inquiry obliterating what had passed, as though nothing had happened.

"Well, now you're *here,*" I said stupidly, rubbing my hands together. "You don't know how happy I am that you're here. Unpack and relax, and I'll be waiting for you downstairs. If you want a drink, the bar is very well stocked."

Talking incoherently, I left the room and went downstairs with my mind in a turmoil. What had caused that sudden collapse, that shocked voice, that look of anguish? I sat on a chaise-longue and closed my eyes. I tried to remember Anne's various expressions: sometimes cold, sometimes affectionate—her moods of irony, easy authority. I found myself both touched and irritated by the discovery that she was vulnerable. Was she in love with my father? Was it possible for her to love him?

He was not at all her type. He was weak, frivolous and sometimes unreliable. But perhaps it was only the fatigue of the trip—or moral indignation. I spent an hour in vain conjecture.

At five o'clock my father and Elsa arrived. I saw him getting out of the car. Again I wondered if Anne could possibly be in love with him. He walked quickly toward me, his head tilted a little backward. He was smiling. Of course it was quite possible for Anne to love him, for anyone to love him!

"Anne wasn't there," he called to me. "I hope she hasn't fallen out of the train?"

"She's in her room," I said. "She came in her car."

"No? Splendid! Then you can take up the bouquet to her!"

"Did you buy me flowers?" called Anne's voice. "How sweet of you!"

She came down the stairs to meet him, cool, smiling, in a dress that showed no signs of travel. I reflected she had appeared only when she heard the car; if she had wanted to talk with me she could have come down earlier—even if only to ask about my exams, in which, by the way, I had failed. This last thought consoled me.

My father rushed up to Anne and kissed her hand.

"I stood a quarter of an hour on the station platform, holding this bunch of flowers, feeling utterly foolish.

Thank goodness you're here! Do you know Elsa Mackenbourg?"

I averted my eyes.

"We must have met," said Anne, all amiability. "What a lovely room you have given me. It was most kind of you to ask me to come here, Raymond. I was exhausted."

My father gave a snort of pleasure. In his eyes everything was going well. He made conversation, uncorked bottles. But I kept thinking, first of Cyril's passionate face, and then of Anne's, both with the stamp of violence on them. And I wondered if the rest of the vacation would be as uncomplicated as my father had assumed.

This first dinner was very gay. My father and Anne talked of the friends they had in common, who were few, but very colorful. I was enjoying myself up to the moment when Anne declared that my father's business partner was an idiot. He was a man who drank a lot, but I liked him very much, and my father and I had had memorable evenings in his company.

"But, Anne," I protested, "Lombard is a lot of fun. He can be very amusing."

"But you've just admitted that he has his faults, and as for his brand of humor—"

"He has perhaps not a very brilliant type of mind, but—"

She interrupted indulgently.

"What you call types of mind are only mental ages."

I was delighted with her remark. Certain phrases

fascinate me with their subtle implications, even though I may not altogether understand their meaning. I told Anne that I wanted to write her comment in my notebook. My father burst out laughing:

"At least you're not resentful!"

How could I be when Anne had not meant to hurt me? I felt that she was impartial, that her judgments did not have the sharp edge of spite. And so they were all the more effective.

The first evening Anne did not seem to notice that Elsa went quite openly into my father's bedroom. She had brought me a sweater she had designed, but would not permit any thanks. It just bored her to be thanked, she said, and as I was awkward in expressing gratitude, I was most relieved.

"I think Elsa is very nice," she remarked as I was about to leave her room to go to bed.

She looked straight at me without a smile, daring me to remember her earlier reaction; I realized I was to forget it.

"Oh yes, she's a charming girl . . . very warm-hearted," I stammered.

She laughed, and I went to bed, most upset. I fell asleep thinking of Cyril who was probably at that moment dancing in Cannes with the same kind of charming girl.

I realize that I have skipped over an important factor: the nearness of the sea with its incessant rhythm. Nor have I mentioned the four lime trees in the courtyard of my convent school and their perfume, or my father's smile as he and I stood at the railroad station three years ago when he came to take me home—his embarrassed smile because my hair was in braids and I wore an ugly, dark dress. And then on the train his sudden, triumphant joy because he saw I had his eyes, his mouth, and I was going to be for him the dearest, most marvelous of toys. I was completely inexperienced; he would show me Paris, luxury, the gay life. I dare say I owed most of my pleasures of that period to money; the pleasure of driving fast in a high-powered car, of buying a new dress, records, books, flowers. Even now I am not ashamed of indulging in these pleasures. In fact I just take them for granted. I would rather deny myself my moods of mysticism or despair than give up my indulgences. My love of pleasure seems to be the only consistent side of my character. Is it because I have not read enough? In school one reads only edifying works. In Paris there was no time for reading; after lectures my boy friends hurried me off to the movies. They were surprised to find that I did not even know the actors' names. I sat with them on sunny café terraces, I savored the pleasure of drifting along with the crowds, of having a drink, of being with a boy who looked deep into my eyes, held my hand, and then led me far away from those same crowds. We would walk slowly home. In the doorway he would draw me close and embrace me; I found out how pleasant it was to be kissed. I don't put names to these memories: Jean,

Hubert, Jacques. They are common in the experiences of all young girls. In the evenings my diversions were more adult; I went to parties with my father. They were very mixed parties, and I was rather out of place, but I enjoyed myself, and the fact that I was so young seemed to amuse everyone. At the end of the evening my father would drop me at our flat, and then see his companion home. I never heard him come in.

I do not want to give the impression that he was vain about his love affairs, but he made no effort to hide them from me, or to invent stories to explain the frequent presence at breakfast of a female friend, not even when she later on became a temporary member of our household. Besides I would soon have discovered the nature of his relations with his "guests," and probably he found it easier to be frank than to take the trouble to deceive me, and thereby lose my confidence. The result, however, was that I adopted a cynical attitude toward love which, considering my age and experience, should have meant happiness rather than mere sensation. I was fond of repeating to myself sayings like Oscar Wilde's:

"Sin is the only note of vivid color that persists in the modern world."

I made this attitude my own with far more conviction, I think, than if I had immediately put it into practice. I believed I could base my life on it, I forgot the bad times, the up and downs, day-to-day happiness. I visualized a life of degradation and moral turpitude as my ideal.

Three

THE NEXT MORNING I was awakened by a slanting ray of hot sunshine that flooded my bed and put an end to my strange and rather confused dreams. Still half asleep, I put my hand up to shield my face from the insistent heat, then gave it up. It was ten o'clock. I went down to the terrace in my pajamas and found Anne glancing through the newspapers. I noticed that she was lightly but perfectly made up; apparently she never allowed herself a real holiday from that. As she paid no attention to me, I sat down on the steps with a cup of coffee and an orange, enjoying the delicious morning. I bit the orange and let its sweet juice run into my mouth, then took a gulp of scalding black coffee and went back to the orange again. The sun warmed my hair and smoothed away the marks of the sheet on my skin. In five minutes I would go for a swim. Anne's voice made me jump.

"Cécile, aren't you eating anything?"

"I like just a drink in the morning."

"To look at all decent you ought to put on six pounds. Your checks are hollow and every rib shows. Do go in and get yourself some bread and butter!"

I begged her not to force me to eat, and she was explaining how important it was, when my father appeared in his luxurious, dotted silk dressing gown.

"What a charming spectacle," he said. "Two little girls sunning themselves and discussing bread and butter."

"Alas, there's only one little girl," said Anne gaily. "Remember I'm your age, my dear Raymond."

My father bent over her and took her hand.

"Still outspoken as ever!" he said tenderly, and I saw Anne's eyelids flutter as if she had received an unexpected caress.

I slipped away unnoticed. On the stairs I passed Elsa. She was obviously just out of bed, with swollen eyelids, pale lips, and her skin red and peeling from too much sun. I almost stopped her to tell her that Anne was already downstairs, her face trim and immaculate—that Anne would be careful to tan slowly and without burning. I thought to put her on her guard, but probably she would have taken it badly. She was twenty-nine, thirteen years younger than Anne, and that seemed to her a trump card.

I got my bathing suit and ran to the cove. To my surprise, Cyril was already there, sitting in his boat. He came to meet me looking serious, took my hands and led me toward the boat.

"I wanted to beg your pardon for yesterday," he said.

"It was my fault," I replied, wondering why he was so solemn.

"I'm very much annoyed with myself," he went on, pushing the boat into the water.

"There's no reason to be," I said lightly.

"But I am!"

I was already in the boat. He was standing in the water up to his knees, resting his hands on the gunwale as if it were the bar of a tribunal. I knew his face well enough to read his expression and I realized that he would not join me until he had said what was on his mind. It made me laugh to think that at the age of twenty-five he still could think of himself as a base seducer.

"Don't laugh," he said. "I really would have gone the whole way, yesterday afternoon. You have no protection against me. Look at the example your father and that woman set you! I might be the most awful cad for all you know."

I did not find him absurd. I saw he was kind, that he was on the verge of real love. I thought it would be nice for me to be in love with him, too. I put my arms around his neck and my cheek against his. He had broad shoulders; his body felt hard against mine.

"You're very sweet, Cyril," I murmured. "You shall be a brother to me."

He pressed his arms around me with an angry little exclamation, and gently pulled me out of the boat. He lifted me up and held me close against him, my head on his shoulder. At that moment I loved him. In the morning light he was as golden, as soft, as gentle as myself, and he would protect me. As his lips touched mine we both began to tremble with pleasure; our kiss was untinged by shame or regret; it was merely a deep searching, interrupted every now and then by whispers. At last I broke away and swam toward the boat, which was drifting out. I dipped my face into the green water to refresh it. A feeling of wild happiness came over me.

At half-past eleven Cyril left, and my father and his two women appeared on the goat path. He was walking between them, offering his hand to each in turn to help them, with a charm and naturalness all his own. Anne was still wearing her beach coat. She removed it with complete unconcern while we all watched her, and lay down on the sand. She had a small waist and perfect legs, and, no doubt as the result of a lifetime of care and attention, her skin was almost without a blemish. Involuntarily I glanced at my father, raising an eyebrow of approval. To my great surprise he did not respond, but instead closed his eyes. Poor Elsa, whose skin was in a lamentable condition, was busy oiling herself. I did not think my father would stand her for another week. . . . Anne turned her head toward me.

"Cécile, why do you get up so early here? In Paris you stayed in bed until midday."

"I was studying then," I said. "That wore me out."

She did not smile. She smiled only when she felt like it, never out of politeness, like other people.

"How did you make out with your examinations?"

"Flunked!" I said, cheerfully. "Completely flunked."

"But you must pass in October, you absolutely *must*!"

"Why should she?" my father interrupted. "I never got any diploma and I manage to live very well."

"You had quite a fortune to start with," Anne reminded him.

"My daughter will always have a man to take care of her," said my father grandiloquently.

Elsa began to laugh, but stopped when she saw our three faces.

"Cécile will have to study during her vacation," said Anne, shutting her eyes to put an end to the conversation.

I gave my father a despairing look but he merely smiled sheepishly. I saw myself in front of an open page of Bergson, its black lines dancing before my eyes, while Cyril was waiting for me at the cove. The idea horrified me. I crept over to Anne and spoke to her in a low voice. She opened her eyes. I bent an anxious, pleading face toward her, drawing in my cheeks to look like an overworked intellectual.

"Anne," I said, "you're not going to make me do

that—make me study in this heat. The rest is doing me so much good!"

She stared at me for a moment, then smiled mysteriously and turned her head away.

"I shall have to make you do *that*, even in this heat, as you say. You'll hold it against me for a day or two, if I know you, but you'll pass your exam."

"There are things one cannot be made to do," I said grimly.

Her only response was a superior smile, and I returned to my place on the beach full of foreboding. Elsa was chattering about various festivities taking place along the Riviera, but my father was not listening. From his place at the apex of the triangle formed by their bodies, he was gazing at Anne's upturned profile with a resolute stare that I recognized. His hand opened and closed on the sand with a gentle, regular, persistent movement. I ran down to the sea and plunged in, bemoaning the gay vacation we might have had. All the elements of a drama were to hand: a libertine, a demimondaine, and a strong-minded woman. I saw an exquisite pink and blue shell on the sea-bottom. I dove for it, and held it, smooth and hollow in my hand all the morning. I decided it was a lucky charm, and that I would keep it. I am surprised that I have not lost it, for I lose everything. Today it is still pink and warm as it lies in my palm, and makes me feel like crying.

Four

ANNE WAS EXTREMELY KIND to Elsa during the following days. In spite of the numerous silly remarks that punctuated Elsa's conversation, Anne never gave vent to any of those sharp phrases which were her specialty, and which would have made poor Elsa ridiculous. I was most surprised, and began to admire Anne's forbearance and generosity, without realizing how subtle she was being. My father would soon have tired of cruel tactics, and he was now so filled with gratitude toward Anne that he could not do enough to please her. He used this gratitude as a means for drawing her, so to speak, into the family circle, suggesting constantly that I was partly Anne's responsibility, and in general behaving toward her as if she were a second mother to me. But I noticed that his every look and gesture betrayed a secret desire for her, a woman whom he had not possessed and whom he longed to enjoy. I had observed a similar gleam in Cyril's eye, and I hesitated between egging him on and running away. In this respect I must have been more susceptible than Anne, for her attitude to my father showed such reserve, such calm friendliness, that I was reassured. I began to believe that I had been mistaken that first day. I was not aware that her engaging frankness was just what excited my father. And then there were her silences, apparently so artless, so sensitive, such a contrast to Elsa's incessant chatter, that it was light and shade. Poor Elsa! She had really no suspicion whatsoever, and, although still suffering from sunburn, remained her usual talkative and exuberant self.

A day came, however, when she must have intercepted a look of my father's and drawn her own conclusions from it. Before lunch I saw her whispering into his ear. For a moment he seemed rather put out, but then he nodded and smiled. After coffee, Elsa walked over to the door, turned around, and struck a languorous, movie-star pose. In her voice was ten years of French coquetry:

"Are you coming, Raymond?"

My father got up, almost blushing, and muttered something about the good to be derived from a nap after a meal as he followed Elsa. Anne had not moved. Her cigarette was smoldering between her fingers. I felt I ought to say something:

"People say that a siesta is restful, but I think it can be quite the reverse . . ."

I stopped short, conscious that my words were equivocal.

"That's enough," said Anne dryly.

There was nothing equivocal about *her* tone. She had, of course, found my remark in bad taste but when I looked at her I saw that she had kept herself calm and composed only with an effort. Perhaps at that very moment she was passionately jealous of Elsa. While I was wondering how I could console her, a cynical idea occurred to me. Cynicism always enchanted me; gave me a delightful feeling of self-assurance and self-approbation. I could not keep it back.

"I imagine that with Elsa's sunburn that kind of siesta can't be much fun for either of them."

I would have done better to keep quiet.

"I detest that kind of remark. At your age it's worse than stupid. It's painful."

I responded angrily: "I only said it as a joke, you know. I'm sure they are really quite happy."

She turned to me with an outraged expression, and I at once apologized. She closed her eyes and began to speak in a low, patient voice.

"Your idea of love is rather primitive. Love is not a series of sensations, each one independent of the others . . ."

I realized that every time I had fallen in love it had been just like that: a sudden emotion, aroused by a face, a gesture or a kiss, . . . thrilling moments, without coherence, was all I remembered.

"It is something different," said Anne. "There are such things as lasting affection, sweetness, a need . . . but I suppose you cannot understand."

She dismissed me with a gesture and took up a newspaper. If only she had been angry instead of resigned to my lack of sentiment. All the same I felt she was right—that I was governed by my instincts like an animal, swayed this way and that by other people that I was shallow and weak. I despised myself, and it was a horribly painful sensation, all the more since I was not used to self-criticism. I went up to my room in a daze. Lying in bed on my warm sheet I thought of Anne's words: "It is something different, it's a need." Had I ever *needed* anyone?

The next fortnight is rather vague in my memory because I deliberately shut my eyes to any threat to our security, but the rest of the vacation stands out clearly because of the role I chose to play in it.

To go back to those first three weeks, three happy weeks on the whole: when was it my father first looked openly at Anne's mouth? Was it the day he reproached her for her aloofness, while pretending to laugh at it? Or the time he solemnly compared her subtlety with Elsa's near-imbecility? My peace of mind was based on the stupid idea that they had known each other for fifteen years, and that if they had been going to fall in love, they would have done so earlier. And I thought also that if it had to happen, the affair would last at the most three months, and Anne would be left with her memories and perhaps a slight feeling of humiliation. Yet all the time I knew in my heart that Anne was not a woman who could be lightly forsaken.

But Cyril was there and filled my thoughts. In the evenings he and I often drove to Saint Tropez and danced in various night clubs to the soft music of a clarinet. At those moments we felt we were madly in love, but by the next morning it was all forgotten. During the day we went sailing. My father sometimes came with us. He thought well of Cyril, especially since Cyril had allowed him to win a swimming race.

He called Cyril "my boy," and Cyril called him "Sir." But I sometimes wondered which of the two was the adult.

One afternoon we went to have tea with Cyril's mother, a quiet smiling old lady who spoke to us of her problems as a widow and mother. My father sympathized with her, looking toward Anne for aid, and paid the old lady innumerable compliments. I must say he never minded giving his time! Anne looked on at the spectacle with an amiable smile, and afterwards said she thought Cyril's mother was charming. I broke into imprecations against old ladies of that sort. Anne and my father laughed at me, which made me furious.

"Don't you realize how pleased she is with herself?" I insisted. "That she pats herself on the back because she feels she has done her duty and . . ."

"But it is true," said Anne. "She has done her duty as a wife and mother, as they say."

"But how about her duty as a mistress?" I asked.

"I don't like vulgarities," Anne said, "even if witty."

"But I'm not trying to be witty. She married the way everyone marries, from desire, or because it's the thing to do. She had a baby—you know where babies come from?"

"Probably not as well as you do," Anne said with irony. "But I have an idea."

"She brought up her child. She probably begrudged herself the bother of a love affair. She had a life like millions of other wives, and she is proud of it, you understand. She had the position of a young, middle-class wife and mother, and she did nothing to jeopardize it. She's pleased with herself for what she hasn't done, not for having accomplished anything."

"That makes no sense," said my father.

"It's like a bird admiring itself," I cried. "She says to herself: 'I did my duty' and she has done nothing. If, with her background, she had become a girl of the streets, that would be worth praising."

"Your ideas are fashionable, but you don't know what you are talking about," Anne said.

She was probably right. At the time, I believed what I said but I must admit that I was only repeating what I had heard. Nevertheless my life and my father's followed my ideas and Anne hurt my feelings by despising them. One can be just as much attached to futilities as to anything else. Anne did not consider me a person with brains. I felt an ardent desire to prove her wrong. I had no idea the opportunity would occur so soon, nor that I would be able to seize it. Anyhow it was quite likely that in a month's time I would have entirely different opinions on any given subject. What more could have been expected of me?

Five

AND THEN ONE DAY things came to a head. In the morning my father said he would like to go to Cannes that evening to dance at the casino, and perhaps gamble as well. I remember how pleased Elsa was. In the familiar casino atmosphere she hoped to resume her role of *femme fatale*, which had been dimmed of late by her sunburn and our semi-isolation. Contrary to my expectation, Anne did not oppose our plans. She even seemed quite pleased. As soon as dinner was over I went up to my room to put on an evening dress, as it happened the only one I possessed. It had been chosen by my father, and was made of an exotic material, probably too exotic for a girl of my age. But my father, either from inclination or habit, liked to have me look sophisticated. I found him downstairs, handsome in a new dinner jacket, and I put my arms around his neck.

"You're the best-looking man I know."

"Except Cyril," he answered insincerely. "And as for you, you're the prettiest girl I know."

"After Elsa and Anne," I replied, also without believing it.

"Since they're not down yet, and have the cheek to keep me waiting, come and dance with your rheumaticky old father!"

Once again I felt the thrill that always preceded our evenings out together. He really had nothing of an old father about him! While dancing I inhaled his familiar odor: a mixture of eau de cologne, warmth and tobacco. He danced slowly, with half-closed eyes, a happy, irrepressible little smile, like my own, on his lips.

"You must teach me the bebop sometime," he said, forgetting his talk of rheumatism.

He stopped dancing to greet Elsa with polite flattery. She came slowly down the stairs in her green dress, a conventional smile on her face, her casino smile. She had made the most of her sun-dried hair and scorched skin, but the result was praiseworthy rather than brilliant. Fortunately she seemed unaware of it.

"Are we off?"

"Anne's not down yet," I remarked.

"Go up and see if she's ready," said my father. "It will be midnight before we get to Cannes."

I ran up the stairs, getting somewhat entangled with my long skirt, and knocked at Anne's door. She called to me to come in, but I stopped on the threshold. She was wearing a gray dress, a very special gray, almost white, which when it caught the light, looked like the sea at dawn. She seemed to me the personification of mature charm. "Oh, Anne, what a magnificent dress!" I said.

She smiled into the mirror as one smiles at a person to whom one is saying good-by.

"This gray *is* a success," she said.

"*You* are a success!" I exclaimed.

She pinched my ear. Her dark-blue eyes lit up with a smile.

"You're a dear child even though you can be irritating at times."

She went out ahead of me without a glance at my dress. In a way I was relieved, but all the same it was mortifying. I followed her down the stairs and I saw my father coming to meet her. He stopped at the bottom, his foot on the first step, his face raised. Elsa was looking on. I remember the scene perfectly. First of all, in front of me, Anne's golden neck and perfect shoulders, a little lower down my father's fascinated face and extended hand, and, off in the background, Elsa's silhouette.

"Anne, you are wonderful!" said my father.

She smiled as she passed him and took her coat.

"Shall we meet at the casino? Cécile, will you come with me?"

She let me drive. At night the road appeared so beautiful that I drove slowly. Anne was silent; she did not even seem to notice the noisy radio. When my father's car passed us at a curve she remained unmoved. I felt I was out of the race, watching a performance in which I could not interfere.

At the casino my father saw to it that we soon lost sight of each other. I found myself at the bar with Elsa and one of her acquaintances, a half-tipsy South American. He was connected with the theater and had such a passionate love for it that even in his drunken condition he could make it interesting. I spent an agreeable hour with him, but Elsa was bored. She liked to hear big names mentioned, but the theater was not her world. Suddenly she asked me where my father was, as if I had some way of knowing. She then left us. The South American seemed put out for a moment, but another whisky set him up again. My mind was a blank. I was quite lightheaded, for I had been drinking with him out of politeness. It became still funnier when he wanted to dance. I was forced to hold him up, and to extricate my feet from under his, which required a lot of agility. We laughed so much that when Elsa tapped me on the shoulder and I saw her Cassandra-like expression, I felt like telling her to go to the devil.

"I can't find them," she said.

She looked utterly distraught. Her powder had worn off, leaving her skin shiny, and her features were drawn. She was a pitiful sight. I suddenly felt very angry with my father; he was being incredibly rude.

"Ah, I know where they are," I said smiling as if everything was as usual and she need have no anxiety. "I'll soon be back."

Deprived of my support, the South American fell in Elsa's arms and seemed quite content there. I reflected somewhat sadly that she was more generously built than I, and I could not hold this against her.

The casino was large, and I went all round it twice without any success. I scanned the terrace and at last thought of the car. It took me some time to find it in the park. They were inside. I approached from behind and saw them through the rear window. Their profiles were very close together, very serious and strangely beautiful in the lamplight. They were facing each other and must have been talking in low tones for I saw their lips move. I would have liked to go away but the thought of Elsa made me open the door. My father had his hand on Anne's arm, and they scarcely noticed me.

"Are you having a good time?" I asked politely.

"What is the matter?" said my father irritably. "What are you doing here?"

"And you? Elsa has been looking for you everywhere for the past hour."

Anne turned her head toward me slowly and reluctantly.

"We're going home. Tell her I was tired and your father had to drive me back. When you've had enough fun, drive my car home."

I was trembling with indignation and could hardly speak.

"Had fun enough? But you don't realize what you're doing! It's disgusting!"

"What is disgusting?" asked my father astonished.

"You take a red-headed girl to the seashore, expose her to the hot sun which she can't stand, and when her skin has all peeled, you abandon her. It's too easy! What on earth shall I say to Elsa?"

Anne turned to him with an air of weariness. He smiled at her, obviously not listening to me. My exasperation knew no bounds.

"I shall tell Elsa that my father has found someone else to sleep with, and that she can call again another time. Is that right?"

My father's exclamation and Anne's slap were simultaneous. I hurriedly withdrew my head from the car door. She had hurt me.

"Apologize at once!" said my father.

I stood motionless and silent with my thoughts in a whirl. Telling retorts always occur to me too late.

"Come here!" said Anne.

She did not sound angry, so I went closer. She put her hand against my cheek and spoke slowly and gently as if I were rather dumb.

"Don't be naughty. I'm very sorry about Elsa, but you are tactful enough to handle her right. Tomorrow we'll discuss it all. Did I hurt you very much?"

"Not at all," I said politely. Her sudden gentleness after my intemperate rage made me want to burst into tears. I watched them drive away, feeling completely deflated. My only consolation was the thought of the tactfulness she had imputed to me.

I walked slowly back to the casino where I found Elsa with the South American clinging to her arm.

"Anne wasn't well," I said in an offhand manner. "Papa had to take her home. How about a drink?"

She looked at me without answering. I tried to find a more convincing explanation.

"She was awfully sick," I said. "It was ghastly, her dress is ruined." This detail seemed to make my story more plausible, but Elsa began to weep quietly and sadly. I did not know what to do.

"Oh, Cécile, we were all so happy!" she said and her sobs redoubled in intensity. The South American began to cry, repeating, "We were so happy, so happy!" At that moment I heartily detested Anne and my father. I would have done anything to stop Elsa from crying, her mascara from running, and the South American from howling.

"Nothing is settled yet, Elsa; come home with me now!"

"No! I'll come and get my suitcase later," she sobbed. "Good-by! We got on well together, didn't we, Cécile?"

We had never talked of anything but clothes or the weather, but still it seemed to me that I was losing an old friend. I quickly turned away and ran to the car.

Six

THE FOLLOWING MORNING I was wretched, probably because of the whisky I had drunk the night before. I awoke in my darkened room to find myself lying across my bed—my tongue heavy, my limbs unbearably damp and sticky. A single ray of sunshine filtered through the slats of the shutters and I could see a million motes dancing in it. I felt no desire to get up, nor to stay in bed. I wondered how Anne and my father would take it if Elsa were to turn up that morning. I forced myself to think of them in order to be able to get out of bed. At last I managed to stand up on my cool, tiled floor. I was giddy and aching.

The mirror reflected a sad sight. I leaned against it and peered at those dilated eyes and dry lips, the face of a stranger. Was that my face? If I was weak and cowardly, could it be because of those lips, the particular shape of my body, these odious, arbitrary physical limitations? And if I were limited, why had I only now become aware of it? I occupied myself by detesting my reflection, hating that wolf-like face, hollow and worn by debauchery. I repeated the word "debauchery" looking into my eyes in the mirror. And then suddenly I saw myself smile. What a great debauch! A few miserable drinks, a slap in the face, and some tears! I brushed my teeth and went downstairs.

My father and Anne were already on the terrace, sitting beside each other at their breakfast tray. I sat down opposite them, muttering a "good morning." A feeling of shyness made me keep my eyes lowered, but after a time, as they remained silent, I was forced to look at them. Anne appeared tired, the only sign of a night of love. They were both smiling happily, and I was very much impressed, for happiness has always seemed to me a great achievement.

"Did you sleep well?" asked my father.

"Not too badly," I replied. "I drank a lot of whisky last night."

I poured out a cup of coffee, but after the first sip I quickly put it down. Their silence had an expectant quality that made me feel uneasy. I was too tired to bear it for long.

"What's the matter? You look so mysterious."

My father lighted a cigarette, making an obvious effort

to seem unconcerned, and for once in her life Anne seemed embarrassed.

"I would like to ask you something," she said at last.

"You want me to take another message to Elsa?" I said, imagining the worst.

She turned toward my father. "Your father and I want to get married," she said.

I stared first at her, then at my father. I half expected some sign from him, perhaps a wink, which, though I might have found it shocking, would have reassured me. But he was looking down at his hands. I said to myself, "It can't be possible!" But I already knew it was true.

"What a good idea," I said to gain time.

I could not understand how my father, who had always set himself so obstinately against marriage and its chains, could have decided on it in a single night. We were about to lose our independence. I could visualize our future family life, a life newly balanced by Anne's intelligence and refinement—the kind of life I had envied her. We would have clever, tactful friends, and quiet pleasant evenings. . . . I found myself despising noisy dinners, South Americans, and girls like Elsa. I felt proud and superior.

"It's a very, very good idea," I repeated, and I smiled at them.

"I knew you'd be pleased, my pet," said my father.

He was relaxed and delighted. Anne's face, subtly

changed by love, seemed gentler, making her more accessible than she had ever been before.

"Come here, my pet," said my father, and holding out his hands, he drew me close to them both. I was half-kneeling in front of them, while they stroked my hair and looked at me tenderly. But I could not keep from thinking that although my life was perhaps at that very moment changing its whole course, I was in reality nothing more than a kitten to them, an affectionate little animal. I felt them above me, united by a past and a future, by ties that I did not know and which could not hold me. But I deliberately closed my eyes and went on playing my part, laying my head on their knees and laughing. For was I not happy? Anne was all right, there was nothing the least mean about her. She would guide me, relieve me of responsibility, and be at hand whenever I might need her. She would make both my father and me into paragons of virtue.

My father went to get a bottle of champagne. My spirits sank. He was happy, which was the chief thing, but I had so often seen him happy on account of a woman.

"I was rather frightened of you," said Anne.

"Why?" I asked. Her words suggested that a veto from me could have stopped their marriage.

"I was afraid of your being frightened of me," she said laughing.

I began to laugh, too, because actually I was a little

scared of her. She wanted me to understand that she knew it, and that I did not need to fear her.

"Does the marriage of two old people like ourselves seem ridiculous to you?"

"You're not old," I said emphatically, as my father came prancing back with a bottle in his hand.

He sat down next to Anne and put an arm around her shoulders. She turned toward him in a way that made me lower my eyes. She was no doubt marrying him for just that; for his laughter, for the firm reassurance of his arm, for his vitality, his warmth. At forty there could be the fear of solitude, or perhaps a final upsurge of the senses. . . . I had never thought of Anne as a woman, but as a personality. I had seen her as a self-assured, elegant, and clever person, but never as weak or sensual. I quite understood that my father felt proud—the proud, reserved Anne Larsen was going to marry him. But did he love her, and if so, was he capable of loving her for long? Was there any difference between this new feeling for her and the feeling he had had for Elsa? The sun was making my head spin, and I shut my eyes. We were all three on the terrace, full of unspoken thoughts, of secret fears, and of happiness.

Elsa did not come back during this time. A week flew by, seven happy, companionable days—and then things changed. While it lasted we made detailed plans for redecorating our Paris flat, and discussed a routine for our life which my father and I took pleasure in elaborating with the blind obstinancy of those who have never had any use for routines. Did he and I ever believe in them for one moment? Did my father really think it possible to have lunch every day at the same place at twelve-thirty sharp, to have dinner at home and spend a quiet evening? Nevertheless he cheerfully prepared to abandon Bohemianism, and began to preach order, to extol the joys of a cultivated, well-organized, bourgeois existence. No doubt for him, as for me, all these plans were just castles in the air.

How well I remember that week! Anne was relaxed, trusting, and very sweet; my father loved her. I saw them coming down in the mornings, leaning on each other, laughing gaily, with shadows under their eyes, and I swear that I should have liked nothing better than that this happiness should last all their lives. In the evening we often drank an apéritif sitting on the terrace of some seaside café. Everywhere we went we were taken for a happy, normal family, and I, who was used to going out alone with my father and seeing the knowing smiles, the malicious or pitying glances, was delighted to play a role more suitable to my age. They were to be married on our return to Paris.

Poor Cyril had witnessed the transformation in our life with a certain amazement, but he was comforted by the thought that this time it would be legalized. We still went sailing together and kissed whenever we felt inclined. But sometimes as he pressed his lips on mine I thought of Anne's face as I saw it every morning, with its softened contours. I recalled the happy ease, the languid grace that love imparted to her movements, and I envied her. Kisses alone can cease to satisfy, and no doubt if Cyril had not been so fond of me, I would have become his mistress that very week.

At six o'clock, on our return from the islands, Cyril would pull the boat onto the sand. We would go up to the house through the pine woods, single file, pretending we were Indians. Or we would run handicap races to warm ourselves up. He always caught me before we reached the house and would spring on me with a shout of victory, rolling me on the pine needles, pinning my arms down and kissing me. I can still remember the taste of those breath-taking kisses, and hear Cyril's heart beating against mine in rhythm with the soft thud of the surf on the beach. One—two—three, his heart pounded out, and one—two—three sounded the waves. Then gradually, as he regained his breath, his kisses would become more urgent, the sound of the sea would grow dim and give way to the pulse beating in my ears.

One evening Anne's voice separated us. Cyril was lying against me. We were half-naked in the red glow of the sunset, and I can understand that Anne might have been deceived by what she saw. She called to me sharply.

Cyril bounded to his feet, naturally somewhat abashed. Keeping my eyes on Anne, I in turn slowly got up. She faced Cyril, and looking right through him, spoke in a quiet voice:

"I don't wish to see you again."

He made no reply, but bent over and kissed my shoulder before departing. I felt surprised and touched, as if his gesture were a sort of pledge. Anne was staring at me with the same grave, detached look, as though she were thinking of something else. Her manner infuriated me. If she were so deep in thought why speak at all? I went up to her, politely pretending to be embarrassed. At last she seemed to notice me and abstractedly removed a pine needle from my neck. I saw her face assume its beautiful mask of disdain, that expression of weariness and superiority which became her so well, and which always frightened me a little.

"You should realize that such diversions usually end up in a hospital."

She stood there looking straight at me as she spoke, and I was horribly ashamed. She was one of those women who can stand perfectly still while they talk. I always needed the support of a chair, or some object to hold, like a cigarette, or the distraction of swinging one leg over the other and watching it move.

"Don't exaggerate," I said with a smile. "I was only kissing Cyril, and that won't lead me to any hospital."

"Please don't see him again," she said, as if she did not believe me. "And don't protest. You are only seventeen and I feel a certain responsibility for you now. I'm not going to let you ruin your life. In any case you have studying to do, and that will take up your afternoons."

She turned her back on me and walked toward the house in her nonchalant way. Shock rooted me to the spot. She had meant every word. What was the use of arguments or denials when she would receive them with the sort of indifference that was worse than contempt, as if I did not even exist, as if I were something to be squashed underfoot, and not myself, Cécile, whom she had always known. My only hope now was my father. Surely he would say as usual: "Well now, what boy is it this time? I hope he's at least handsome and healthy. But keep away from the wolves, my girl!" If he did not react like this, my vacation would be ruined.

Dinner was a nightmare. Not for a moment had Anne intimated to me that she would not be a tattle-tale and tell my father about it if I would promise to study. It was not in her nature to bargain. In a way I approved of her as she was, but still I would have liked some action from her that would give me a chance to despise her. As usual she avoided a false move, and it was only when we had finished our soup that she seemed to remember the incident.

"I do wish you'd give your daughter some advice, Raymond. I came across her in the woods with Cyril this evening, and they seemed to be going rather far."

My father, poor man, tried to pass the whole thing off as a joke.

"What's that you say? What were they up to?"

"He was kissing me," I said, "and Anne thought . . ."

"I never thought anything at all," she interrupted. "But it might be a good idea for her to stop seeing him for a time and to work at her philosophy instead."

"Oh, the poor little thing!" said my father. "After all, Cyril's a nice boy, isn't he?"

"And Cécile is a nice girl," said Anne. "That's why I should be heartbroken if anything should happen to her, and it seems to me inevitable that it will if she continues to have such complete freedom. She and Cyril are constantly together and both are completely idle. So what can one expect? Don't you agree?"

At her last words I lifted my eyes and my father lowered his, very embarrassed.

"You are probably right," he said. "After all, you ought to do some work, Cécile. You surely don't want to fail in philosophy and have to take it again?"

"What do you think I care?" I answered sharply.

He glanced at me and then turned away. I was bewildered. I realized that carelessness can govern our lives, but it does not provide us with any arguments in its defense.

"Listen," said Anne, taking my hand across the table. "Won't you drop your role of a wood nymph and become a good schoolgirl for just one month? Would that be so hard?"

They both looked at me, smiling affectionately. Seen

in that light, the argument was obvious. I gently withdrew my hand.

"Yes, very hard," I said so softly that they did not hear it, or did not want to.

The following morning I came across a paragraph from Bergson. It took me several minutes to understand it:

"Whatever irrelevance one may at first find between the cause and the effects, and although a rule of guidance towards an assertion concerning the root of things may be far distant, it is always in a contact with the generative force of life that one is able to extract the power to love humanity."

I repeated the paragraph, quietly at first, so as not to get agitated, then in a louder voice. I held my head in my hands and looked at the words intently. At last I understood it, but I felt as cold and impotent as when I had read it the first time. I simply could not go on with my reading. With the best will in the world I applied myself to the next lines, but suddenly something arose in me like a storm and threw me onto the bed. I thought of Cyril waiting for me down in the golden cove, of the gently swaying boat, of the taste of our kisses, and I I thought of Anne, but in a way that made me sit up on my bed with a fast-beating heart, telling myself that I was stupid, monstrous, nothing but a lazy, spoiled child, and had no right to have such thoughts. But just the same, in spite of myself, I went on thinking that she was a danger to me, and that I must get rid of her. I thought of the dinner I had endured with clenched teeth, tortured by a feeling of resentment for which I despised and ridiculed myself.

Yes, it was this I held against Anne: she kept me from liking myself. I, who was naturally meant for happiness and gaiety, had been forced by her into self-criticism and a guilty conscience. Unaccustomed to introspection, I was completely lost. And what good did she do me? I took stock: she wanted my father; she had got him. She would gradually turn us into the husband and stepdaughter of Anne Larsen, that is to say, she would turn us into two civilized, well-behaved and contented persons. For she would certainly be good to us. How easily—unstable and irresponsible as we were—we would yield to her influence, and be fitted into the attractive framework of her orderly plan of living. She was much too efficient. Already my father was separated from me. I was hurt by his embarrassed face, turning away from me at the table. Tears came into my eyes at the thought of the jokes we used to have together, our gay laughter as we drove home at dawn through the deserted streets of Paris. All that was over. In my turn I would be influenced, readjusted, remodeled by Anne. I would not even mind it, she would handle me with such intelligence, humor and sweetness. I wouldn't be able to resist her. In six months I should no longer even want to.

At all costs I must save myself, regain my father and

our former life. How infinitely charming those two years with him now seemed, those gay times I was so ready to give up just the other day . . . the freedom to think for myself, even to think wrongly or not at all, the freedom to choose my own life, to choose myself. I cannot say I wanted to "be myself," for I knew I was still soft clay. But I refused to be molded.

I realize that some people might find complicated motives for this revolt in me. Some might endow me with startling complexes: such as an incestuous love for my father, or a morbid passion for Anne. But I know the true reasons were the heat, Bergson and Cyril, or rather Cyril's absence. My thoughts went on all the afternoon. I was in a most unpleasant mood, brought on by the discovery that we were entirely at Anne's mercy. I was not used to reflection, and it made me irritable. At dinner, as in the morning, I did not open my mouth. My father finally attempted a little teasing:

"What I like about youth is its spontaneity, its gay conversation."

I was trembling with rage. It was true that he loved youth; and with whom could I have talked if not with him? We had discussed everything together: love, death, music. Now he himself had silenced me, abandoned me. Looking at him I thought: "You don't love me any more, you have betrayed me!" I tried to make him understand without words how desperate I was. I gave myself up completely to hysteria. Suddenly he seemed to sense it;

perhaps he understood that the time for joking was past, and that our relationship was in danger. I saw him stiffen, and he seemed about to speak to me. Anne turned to me:

"You don't look well. I'm sorry now I made you study."

I did not reply. I felt too disgusted that I had got myself into a state which I could no longer control. We had finished dinner. On the terrace, in the rectangle of light projected from the dining-room window, I saw Anne's long nervous hand reach out to find my father's. I thought of Cyril. I would have liked him to take me in his arms on that terrace, flooded with moonlight and the noise of the crickets. I would have liked to be caressed, consoled, reconciled with myself. My father and Anne were silent. They had a night of love to look forward to; I had Bergson. I tried to cry, to feel sorry for myself, but in vain. Already I was sorry for Anne, as if I were certain that I would conquer her.

Part Two

One

HOW CLEARLY I REMEMBER everything from that moment on! I acquired an added awareness of other people and of myself. An unthinking, easy egoism had been natural to me. I had always lived like this. But the last few days had upset me deeply, forcing me to reflect, to look at myself with a critical eye. I endured all the pangs of introspection, and still couldn't become reconciled with myself. "These feelings," I thought, "these feelings about Anne are mean and stupid; this desire to separate her from my father is vicious." But after all, why was I so hard on myself? Wasn't I free to judge what happened? For the first time in my life my "self" seemed to be split, and I discovered opposing forces within that shocked me. I found good excuses, I whispered them to myself, trying to be honest, and suddenly another "me" rose up which answered all my arguments, saying that I was fooling myself with them, although they had all the appearance of truth. But truly, wasn't it this other "me" who was wrong? Wasn't this clear-headedness my worst mistake? Up in my room I reasoned with myself for hours on end in an attempt to discover whether the fear and hostility which Anne inspired in me were justified, or if I was merely a silly, spoiled, selfish girl pretending to be adult.

In the meantime I grew thinner every day. On the beach I did nothing but sleep, and at mealtimes I maintained a strained silence that finally made the others uneasy.

And all the time I watched Anne. At dinner I would say to myself, "Everything she does shows how much she loves him. Could anyone be more in love? How can I be angry with her when she smiles at me with that worried look in her eyes?" But then she would say, "When we get back home to Paris, Raymond . . ." And the thought that she was going to share our life and interfere with us would anger me again. Again she seemed calculating and cold. I thought: "She is cold, we are warm-hearted. She is dictatorial, we are easy-going. She is standoffish; other people don't interest her though we love them. She is reserved; we are gay. Here we are, the two of us, and she will glide in between us quietly. She will warm herself at our fire and gradually absorb our carefree warmth. She will have us in her coils, like a beautiful serpent," I repeated, "just like a beautiful serpent." Then Anne passed me the bread, and suddenly I came to my senses. "But I'm crazy," I thought. "That's Anne, your friend who was so kind to you, who is so clever. Her aloofness is a mere habit, there's nothing calculated about it. Her reserve is just to shield her from countless sordid things in life. It's a sign of nobility. A beautiful serpent . . ." I felt myself turn pale with shame. I looked at her, silently imploring her forgiveness. At times she noticed my expression and a shadow of surprise and concern would cloud her face and make her break off in the middle of a sentence. Then her eyes would turn instinctively to my father; but his glance never showed anything but admiration or desire. He did not understand the cause of her disquiet. Little by little I made the atmosphere unbearable, and I detested myself for it.

My father suffered as much as his nature permitted, that is to say, hardly at all, for he was mad about Anne, intensely proud and happy, and nothing else existed for him. However, one day when I was dozing on the beach after my morning swim, he sat down next to me and looked at me closely. I felt his eyes upon me, and with my air of false gaiety that was fast becoming a habit, I was about to ask him to come in for a swim when he put his hand on my head and called to Anne in a doleful voice:

"Come over here and have a look at this little creature. She's as thin as a rail. If this is the effect studying has on her, she'll have to give it up!"

He thought that would settle everything, and no doubt

it would have done so ten days earlier. But by now I was too deeply immersed in complications, and the hours set aside for work in the afternoons no longer bothered me, especially as I had not opened a book since Bergson.

Anne came up to us. I remained lying face down on the sand, listening to the muffled sound of her footsteps. She sat on my other side.

"It certainly doesn't seem to agree with her," she said. "But if she really did some work instead of walking up and down in her room . . ."

I had turned around and was looking at them. How did she know that I was not studying? Perhaps she could even read my thoughts? I thought her capable of anything. It frightened me. I protested.

"I don't walk up and down in my room!"

"Are you lonesome for that boy?" asked my father.

"No!"

This was not quite true, but I certainly had had no time to think of Cyril.

"But still, you're not well," said my father firmly. "Anne, look at her. She looks like a chicken that has been plucked and put to roast in the sun."

"Cécile, dear," said Anne, "try to pull yourself together. Do just a little work and eat a great deal. That exam *is* important . . ."

"I don't care a hang about the exam!" I cried. "Can't you understand? I just don't care!"

I looked straight at her, despairingly, so that she

should realize that something more serious than an exam was at stake. I longed for her to ask me, "Well, what *is* the matter?" and to ply me with questions, force me to tell her everything. Then I would be won over and she could do anything she liked with me, and I should no longer be in torment. She looked at me attentively. I could see the deep blue of her eyes darken with concentration and reproach. Then I understood that it would never occur to her to ply me with questions and so deliver me from myself, because even if the thought had entered her head, her code of behavior would have forbidden it. And I saw, too, that she had no idea of the tumult within me. Or even if she did, I thought, she would have withdrawn in disdain and disapproval, which was exactly what I deserved! Anne always gave everything its exact value; that is why I could never come to an understanding with her.

I dropped back onto the sand and laid my cheek against its soft warmth. I sighed deeply and began to tremble. I could feel Anne's hand, tranquil and steady, on the back of my neck, holding me still for a moment, just long enough to stop my nervous tremor. "Don't complicate life for yourself," she said. "You've always been so contented and lively, so thoughtless. And here you are now, sad and introspective. It doesn't suit you."

"I know," I answered. "I'm just a thoughtless, healthy child, gay and silly!"

"Come and have lunch," she said.

My father had moved away from us; he hated that sort

of discussion. On the way back he took my hand and held it. His hand was firm and comforting; it had dried my tears after my first disappointment in love, it had closed over mine in moments of peace and perfect happiness, it had stealthily pressed mine at times when we were misbehaving, or laughing riotously. I thought of his hand on the steering wheel, or holding the door keys at night and searching in vain for the lock; his hand on a woman's shoulder, or holding a cigarette—the hand that could do nothing more for me. I gave it a hard squeeze. Turning toward me, he smiled.

Two

TWO DAYS WENT BY. I went around in circles, wearing myself out, but I could not free myself from the haunting thought that Anne was about to wreck our lives. I did not try to see Cyril. He could have comforted me and made me happier, but that was not what I wanted. I even got a certain satisfaction from asking myself unanswerable questions, by reminding myself of days gone by, and dreading those to come. It was very hot. I kept my room in semidarkness with the shutters closed, but even so the air was unbearably heavy and damp. I lay on my bed staring at the ceiling, moving only to search for a cooler place on the sheet. I could not sleep. Frequently I played records on the phonograph at the foot of my bed. I chose slow rhythms, without a melody. I smoked a good deal and felt decadent, which gave me pleasure. But I was not deluded by this game of pretense: I was sad and bewildered.

One afternoon the maid knocked at my door and announced with an air of mystery: "Someone's downstairs." I at once thought of Cyril and went down. It was not Cyril, but Elsa. She greeted me effusively. Looking at her, I was astonished at her new beauty. She was marvelously tanned at last, evenly and smoothly, and was carefully made up and brilliantly youthful.

"I've come to get my suitcase," she explained. "Juan bought me a few dresses, but not enough, and I need my things."

I wondered for a moment who Juan could be, but did not inquire further. I was pleased Elsa had come back. She brought with her the aura of a kept woman, of bars, of gay evenings, which reminded me of happier days. I told her how glad I was to see her again, and she assured me that we had always got on so well together because we had common interests. I suppressed a slight shudder and suggested that we should go up to my room to avoid meeting Anne and my father. When I mentioned my father her head jerked involuntarily and I wondered whether she was still in love with him, in spite of Juan and the dresses. I also thought that three weeks before I would not have noticed that movement of her head.

In my room I listened while she described in glowing terms her smart and giddy life in the fashionable places along the Riviera. A strange confusion of thoughts went through my head, partly suggested by her improved appearance. At last she stopped talking, perhaps because I was silent. She took a few steps across the room, and without turning round, asked in an offhand way, "Is Raymond happy?" In a moment I realized what I must say to her.

" 'Happy' is saying too much. Anne doesn't give him a chance to think he isn't happy. She is very clever."

"Very!" sighed Elsa.

"You'll never guess what she's persuaded him to do! She's going to marry him . . ."

Elsa turned a horrified face toward me.

"Marry him? Raymond actually wants to get *married*?"

"Yes," I answered. "Raymond is going to be married."

A sudden desire to laugh caught me by the throat. My hands were shaking. Elsa seemed prostrated, almost as if I had struck her. I must not let her entertain the idea that he had reached the age when marriage was suitable, that he could not be expected to spend the rest of his life with demimondaines. I leaned forward and lowered my voice to make a stronger impression on her.

"It simply mustn't happen, Elsa. He's suffering already. It's an impossible state of affairs, as you can very well imagine."

"Yes," she said. She seemed fascinated by my words.

"You're just the person I've been waiting for," I went on. "Because you are the only one who is a match for Anne. You alone are up to her standard."

She seemed to swallow the bait. "But if he's marrying her it must be because he loves her!" she objected.

"But look here, Elsa, it's you he loves! Don't try to tell me you don't know it."

She blinked her eyelids, and turned away to hide the pleasure and the hope my words had given her. I was in a kind of hypnotic state, but I knew just what I should say to her.

"Don't you see? Anne kept harping on the bliss of married life, and all that, and in the end she caught him."

I was surprised at my own words. For even though I had expressed myself somewhat crudely, that was indeed what I thought.

"If they get married, our three lives will be ruined, Elsa! My father must be protected. He's nothing but a big baby."

I repeated "a big baby" with stronger emphasis. It occurred to me that I might be overdoing my melodrama, but then I saw Elsa's beautiful green eyes fill with pity, and I wound up, as in a litany:

"Help me, Elsa! Give me aid! For your own sake! For the sake of my father! And for the love you bear each other!"

I added *sotto voce*: "And for the sake of John Chinaman!"

"But what can I *do*?" pleaded Elsa. "There seems no way out!"

"If you think there's no way out, then forget about it," I sadly said.

"What a bitch she is!" murmured Elsa.

"You've hit the nail on the head," I said, turning away to hide my satisfaction.

Elsa visibly brightened up. Her ideas poured forth. She had been jilted, she said, and now she was going to show that adventuress just what she, Elsa Mackenbourg, could do. And of course my father loved her; she had always known he loved her. Even while she had been with Juan she hadn't been able to put Raymond out of her mind. She'd never as much as mentioned the word marriage to Raymond, and she had always given him a good time. And she would never even try to. . . . But by now I could endure her no longer. "Elsa," I said, "go to Cyril and ask him as a favor to me if you could possibly stay with his mother. Say you are in need of hospitality. I'm sure he can get his mother to do it. Tell him I'll come to see him tomorrow morning, and the three of us will discuss the situation."

On the doorstep, meaning to be funny, I added: "You are fighting for your future, Elsa!"

She gravely acquiesced as if there were not fifteen or twenty futures in store for her, in the shape of men who would support her. I watched her walking away in the sunshine with her mincing steps. I thought that, before a week had gone by, my father would want her back.

It was then three-thirty. At this moment my father must have been sleeping in Anne's arms, and she too, blooming, weary, filled with the heat of pleasure and happiness, must have given herself to sleep. I began to formulate plans one after another, without pausing to reflect. I walked up and down in my room between the door and the window, looking out from time to time at the calm sea stretched out along the beach. I calculated the risks, estimated possibilities, and gradually I overcame every objection. I felt menacingly clever, and the wave of self-disgust which had swept over me when I first spoke to Elsa now gave place to a feeling of pride in my own capabilities.

I need hardly say that this collapsed when we all went down to swim. As soon as I saw Anne, I was overcome by remorse and did my utmost to atone for my past misbehavior. I carried her bag, I rushed forward with her wrap when she came out of the water. I smothered her with attentions and said the nicest things. This sudden change after my silence of the past few days naturally surprised her. My father was delighted. Anne smiled at me and became very gay. I thought of the words I had used in speaking of her to Elsa. How could I have said them, and how could I have put up with Elsa's nonsense? Tomorrow I would advise Elsa to go away, saying that I had made a mistake. Everything would be as before, and, after all, why should I not try to pass my examination? A college degree was sure to come in useful later on.

"Isn't that so?" I asked Anne. "Isn't it useful to get a college degree?"

She gave me a look and burst out laughing. I followed suit, happy to see her so gay. "You're really incredible!" she exclaimed.

I certainly was incredible, and she would have thought me even more so if she had known what I had been planning. I was dying to tell her all about it so that she should see how incredible I could be. I wanted to tell her: "Can you imagine that I was going to make Elsa pretend to be in love with Cyril? She was to go and stay in his house, and we would have seen them sailing by in his boat, strolling in the woods or along the road. Elsa looks lovely again. Of course she hasn't your beauty. Hers is the flamboyant kind that makes men turn around. My father wouldn't have stood it for long. He could never allow a good-looking woman who had lived with him to take another lover so soon and, so to speak, right before his eyes, and certainly not a man younger than himself. You understand, Anne, he would have wanted her again very quickly even though he loves you, just in order to bolster his morale. He's very vain, or else not very sure of himself, whichever way you like to put it. Elsa, under my direction, would have done all that was necessary. The day would surely come when he would have been unfaithful to you. And you couldn't bear that, could you? You're not one of those women who can share a man. So you would have gone away. And that was exactly what I wanted. It's stupid, I know, but I was angry with you because of Bergson, because of the heat. I somehow imagined . . . I daren't even tell you, it was so ridiculous and unreal. On account of my college exam I might have caused a complete break with you—you, the old friend of my mother, *our* friend . . . And it *is* useful, isn't it, to have a college degree?" Then: "Isn't it?" I said aloud.

"Isn't *what?*" asked Anne. "That a degree is useful?"

"Yes," I replied.

After all, it was better not to tell her anything; perhaps she could not have understood. There were things Anne did not understand at all. I ran into the sea behind my father and wrestled playfully with him. Once more I was able to enjoy frolicking in the water, for now I had a good conscience. Tomorrow I would change my room; I would move up to the attic with my schoolbooks. But Bergson would not be among them; there was no need to overdo it! For two hours every day I would concentrate in solitude on my work. I imagined myself triumphantly passing the examinations in October, and thought of my father's astonished laugh, Anne's approbation, my degree. I would be intelligent, cultured, somewhat aloof, like Anne. Perhaps I had intellectual gifts? Hadn't I been capable of producing a sound, logical plan, despicable perhaps, but logical? And what about Elsa? I had known how to appeal to her vanity and sentimentality, and within a few minutes had managed to persuade her, when her only object in coming back had been to get her suitcase. I felt proud of myself: I had sized up Elsa, found her weak spot, and carefully aimed my words. For the first time in my life I had known the intense pleasure of analyzing another person, manipulating that person toward my own ends. It was a new experience; in the past I had always been too impulsive, and whenever I had come close to understanding someone, it had been pure accident. Now I had caught a sudden glimpse of the marvelous mechanism of human reflexes, and the power that lies in the spoken word. I felt sorry that I had come to it through lies. The day might come when I would love someone passionately, and would have to search warily, gently for the way to reach his heart.

Three

WALKING DOWN TO Cyril's villa the next morning, I felt far less sure of my intellectual prowess. To celebrate my recovery, I had drunk too much at dinner the night before, and had been rather more than gay. I had told my father that I was going to work for a degree, and would associate in future only with highbrows; that I wanted to become famous and a thorough bore. I said he must make use of every scandalous trick known to publicity in order to launch my career. Roaring with laughter, we said the wildest things. Anne laughed, too, but indulgently and not so loudly. When I became too extravagant, she stopped laughing altogether. But our hilarious fun had put my father into such a happy frame of mind that she did not try to stop it. At last they went to bed, after tucking me in. I thanked them from the bottom of my heart, and said what would

I ever do without them. My father had no answer, but Anne looked as if she were about to express very decided views on the subject. Just as she leaned over to speak to me, I fell asleep. In the middle of the night I was sick, and my awakening the next morning was the worst I could ever remember. Still feeling very fuzzy and in low spirits, I walked slowly toward the woods, having no eyes for the sea or for the restless seagulls.

Cyril was at his garden gate. He rushed toward me, took me in his arms, and held me tightly, talking incoherently.

"I was so worried! Oh, darling! It's been so long! I had no idea what you were doing, or if that woman was making you suffer. I've never been so miserable. Several times I hung around your cove all afternoon, hoping . . . I had no idea how much I loved you!"

"Neither did I," I said.

To tell the truth, I was both surprised and touched, but I could not express my feelings because I had such a hangover.

"How pale you are!" he said. "From now on I'm going to look after you. I won't let you be ill-treated any more."

I recognized Elsa's exaggerations and asked Cyril what his mother thought of Elsa.

"I introduced her as a friend of yours, an orphan. As a matter of fact, she's very nice; she told me all about *that woman*. How strange it is that with such a delicate, refined face she could be such a low adventuress."

"Elsa is too sensational," I said weakly. "But I am on my way to tell her . . ."

"I, too, have something to tell *you*," interrupted Cyril. "Cécile, I want to marry you."

I had a moment of panic. I absolutely had to do or say something. If only I did not have this dreadful hangover!

"I love you," said Cyril, speaking into my hair. "I'll give up studying law. An uncle of mine has offered me an interesting job. I'm twenty-six. I'm not a boy any longer. I am serious about this. What do you say?"

I tried desperately to think of a noncommittal, high-sounding phrase. I did not want to marry him. I loved him, yes, but I did not want to marry him. I didn't want to marry anyone; I was tired.

"It's quite impossible," I stammered. "My father . . ."

"I'll manage your father," said Cyril.

"Anne wouldn't approve," I said. "She doesn't think I'm grown up. If she says no, my father will say the same. I'm *so* exhausted, Cyril. All this emotion wears me out. Here's Elsa!"

She was wearing a negligee, and looked fresh and radiant. I was spiritless, emaciated. Both Cyril and Elsa were overflowing with health and high spirits, which depressed me even more. She treated me as though I had just escaped from jail, fussed over me. I sat down.

"How is Raymond?" she asked. "Does he know I'm here?"

She had the happy smile of one who has forgiven and is full of hope. How could I tell her that my father had forgotten her existence? How explain to Cyril that I did not want to marry him? I shut my eyes. Cyril went to get some coffee. Elsa talked on and on. She obviously thought me a very subtle person on whom she could count completely. The coffee was strong and fragrant. The sun was good and hot. I began to feel a little better.

"I've thought and thought, but without finding a way out," said Elsa.

"There isn't one," said Cyril. "Your father is infatuated, there's nothing to be done."

"Oh yes, there is!" I said. "You just haven't any imagination."

It flattered me to see how they hung on my words. They were ten years older than I, and still they had no ideas! I said with a superior air: "It is a question of psychology."

I went on to explain my plan. They raised the same objections I had raised to myself the day before and I felt a particular pleasure in refuting them. I got excited all over again, in my effort to convince them that my plan was feasible. When it came to proving why it ought not to be carried out, my arguments were not so logical.

"I don't like that kind of intrigue," said Cyril reluctantly. "But if it is the only way to make you marry me, I'll do it."

"That's not entirely up to Anne," I said.

"You know very well that if she stays, you'll have to marry the man she chooses," said Elsa.

Perhaps that was true. I could see Anne introducing me on my twentieth birthday to a young man with a college degree to match my own, assured of a brilliant future, steady and faithful. In fact, someone like Cyril himself! I began to laugh.

"Please don't laugh," said Cyril. "Tell me that you'll be jealous when I'm pretending to be in love with Elsa. How can you bear the thought of it for one moment? Do you love me?"

He spoke in a low voice. Elsa had gone off discreetly and left us alone. I looked at Cyril's tense, brown face, his dark eyes. It gave me a strange feeling to think he loved me. I looked at his red lips, so near mine. I did not feel intellectual any longer. He came closer, our lips met and he kissed me passionately. I stayed seated, eyes open, his mouth against mine, hot and hard. A light tremor ran through me. He paused a minute, then his lips opened and our kiss became quickly imperious, skilled, too skilled. I realized that I was more gifted in kissing a young man in the warm sunshine than in taking a degree. I drew away from him, gasping for breath.

"Cécile, we've got to live together, forever! Meanwhile, I'll play the game with Elsa."

I wondered if I was right in my reckoning. Since I was

the instigator of the whole thing, I thought, I could always stop it.

"You're so full of ideas," said Cyril with his special smile that lifted one side of his mouth and gave him the appearance of a handsome brigand.

And that is how I set the whole drama in motion, against my better judgment. Sometimes I think I would blame myself less if I had been prompted that day by hatred and violence, and had not allowed myself to drift into it merely through inertia, the sun, and Cyril's kisses.

When I left my fellow conspirators at the end of an hour, I was rather perturbed. However, there were still grounds for reassurance; my plan might well misfire because my father's real passion for Anne would keep him faithful to her. In addition, neither Cyril nor Elsa could do much without my connivance. If my father showed any signs of falling into the trap, I could find some means of putting an end to the whole thing. But still it was amusing to try the plan out, and see whether my psychological judgment proved right or wrong.

Moreover, Cyril was in love with me and had asked me to marry him. This was enough to put me into a pleasant daze. If he could wait two years, to give me time to grow up, I would accept him. I could already imagine myself living with Cyril, sleeping next to him, never leaving him. Every Sunday we would go to lunch with Anne and my father, a happy married couple, and sometimes perhaps we would include Cyril's mother, which would add the final touch of domesticity.

I met Anne on the terrace on her way down to the beach to join my father. She received me with that teasing smile with which one greets those who have drunk too much the night before. I asked her what she had been going to say to me just as I fell asleep, but she only laughed and said it might make me cross. Just then my father came out of the water. He was broad and muscular, and I thought he looked wonderful. I went into the water with Anne, who swam slowly with her head well out of the water so she wouldn't wet her hair. Afterward we three lay side by side on our stomachs in the sand, with me in the middle. We were quiet and peaceful.

Just then a boat appeared around the rocks, all sails set. My father was the first to see it.

"So Cyril couldn't hold out any longer!" he said laughing. "Shall we forgive him, Anne? After all, he's a nice boy."

I raised my head, scenting danger.

"But what is he up to?" said my father. "He's not coming in, after all. Ah! He's not alone."

Anne had also turned to look. The boat was passing right in front of our beach, before tacking. I could make out Cyril's features. Silently I prayed that he would disappear, but then I heard my father's exclamation of surprise:

"But it's Elsa! What on earth is she doing there?"

He turned to Anne. "That girl is incredible! She must already have got her claws into that poor boy and made the old lady tolerate her."

But Anne was not listening; she was watching me. I saw her and hid my face in the sand to cover my shame. She put out her hand and touched my neck.

"Look at me. Do you blame me for it?"

I opened my eyes. She bent over me anxiously, almost imploringly. For the first time she was treating me as a sensible person with feelings just on the day when. . . . I groaned and jerked my head around toward my father to free myself from her hand. He was watching the boat.

"My poor child," Anne was saying in a low voice, "poor little Cécile! I'm afraid it is all my fault. Perhaps I shouldn't have been so hard on you. I never wanted to hurt you. Do you believe me?"

She gently stroked my hair and neck. I kept quite still. I had the same physical sensation as when a receding wave dragged the sand away from under me. Neither anger nor desire had ever worked so strongly in me as my longing at that moment for utter defeat. My one wish was to give up all my plans and put myself entirely into her hands for the rest of my life. I had never before been so overcome with such a sense of utter impotence. I closed my eyes. It seemed to me that my heart stopped beating.

Four

So far my father had shown no feeling other than surprise. Back at the house, the maid told him that Elsa had been to get her suitcase, but said nothing about her visit with me. Being a peasant woman with a romantic turn of mind, she must have relished the various changes that had taken place in our household since she had been with us, especially in the bedrooms.

My father and Anne, in their effort to make amends, were so kind to me that at first I found it unbearable. However, I soon changed my mind, for even though I had brought it on myself, I did not find it very agreeable to see Cyril and Elsa walking about arm in arm, showing every sign of pleasure in each other's company. I could no longer go sailing with him myself, but I had to watch Elsa passing by, her hair blown by the wind, as mine used to be. It was easy enough for me to look coldly away whenever we met, as we frequently did: in the woods, in the village, and on the road. Anne would glance at me, start a new topic of conversation, and put her hand on my shoulder to comfort me. Have I mentioned before how kind she could be? Whether her kindness emanated from her intelligence, or was merely part of her self-control, I do not know. But she had an unerring instinct for the right, tactful word. If I had really been unhappy over Cyril, I could hardly have found better consolation.

As my father gave no sign of jealousy, I was as yet not unduly worried, so I let things drift. But while it proved to me how fond he was of Anne, I felt rather annoyed that my plan had misfired. One day he and I were on our way to the post office when we passed Elsa. She pretended not to see us, and my father turned after her with a whistle of surprise, as if she had been a stranger.

"I say! Hasn't she become a beauty?"

"Love seems to agree with her," I remarked.

He looked surprised. "You're taking it very well, I must say!"

"What can one expect? Cyril and Elsa are about the same age. I suppose it was inevitable."

"If Anne hadn't come along, it wouldn't have been inevitable at all!" he said angrily. "You don't think I'd let a boy like that snatch a woman from me unless I didn't care?"

"All the same, age counts!" I said solemnly.

He shrugged his shoulders. On the way back I noticed he was preoccupied. Perhaps he was thinking that both Cyril and Elsa were young, and that in marrying a woman of his own age, he would cease to belong to the age group of men who are looked upon as still young. I had a momentary feeling of triumph, but when I saw the tiny wrinkles at the corners of Anne's eyes, and the fine lines around her mouth, I felt ashamed of myself. It was only too easy to follow my impulses and repent afterward.

A week went by. Cyril and Elsa, who had no idea how matters were progressing, must have been expecting me every day. I was afraid to go and see them for fear I would be tempted to try something else. Every afternoon I went up to my room, ostensibly to study, but in fact I did nothing. I found a book on Yoga and spent my time practicing various exercises. I took care to smother my laughter in case Anne should hear. I told her I was working hard. I pretended that my disappointment in love had made me keen to get my degree as a consolation. I hoped this would raise me in her estimation, and I even went so far as to quote Kant at table, to my father's dismay.

One afternoon I had wrapped myself in bath towels to look like a Hindu, and was sitting cross-legged staring at myself in the mirror, hoping to achieve a Yoga-like trance, when there was a knock at the door. I thought it was the maid and told her to come in.

It was Anne. For a moment she remained transfixed in the doorway, then she smiled.

"What are you playing at?"

"Yoga," I replied, "But it's not a game at all. It's a Hindu philosophy."

She went to the table and took up my book. I began to be worried. It was open at page one hundred and the preceding pages were covered with remarks in my handwriting, such as "too hard" or "exhausting."

"You are certainly conscientious," she said. "And what about that essay you're writing on Pascal? I don't see it anywhere."

At lunch I had been talking about Pascal, implying that I was working on a certain passage, but, needless to say, I had not written a word. Anne waited for me to say something, but as I did not reply, she understood.

"It is your own business if you play the fool up here instead of working, but it's quite another matter when you lie to your father and me. I must admit it was hard to believe in this sudden intellectual activity."

She went out of the room, leaving me petrified in my bath towels. I could not understand why she had used the word "lie." I had spoken of Pascal because it amused me, and had mentioned my essay to make her happy, and now she blamed me for it. I had grown used to her new, tolerant attitude toward me, and her contempt made me feel humiliated and furious. I threw off my disguise, pulled on some slacks and an old shirt and rushed out of the house.

The heat was terrific, but I began to run, impelled by my anger, which was all the more violent because it was mixed with shame. I ran all the way to Cyril's villa, stopping only when I reached his door to regain my breath. In the afternoon heat, the house seemed unnaturally large and quiet, full of secrets. I crept silently up to Cyril's room; he had showed it to me the day we called on his mother. I opened the door. Cyril was lying across the bed, fast asleep with his head on his arm. I stood looking at him. For the first time he seemed vulnerable and rather touching. I called to him in a low voice. He opened his eyes and sat up at once.

"You, Cécile! What's the matter?"

I signed to him not to talk so loudly. Suppose his mother were to come and find me in his room? She might think . . . wouldn't anyone think . . . ? Suddenly I felt panic-stricken and moved toward the door.

"But don't go away!" he cried. "Come here, Cécile!"

He caught me by the wrist and, laughing, kept me from moving. I turned around to him and saw him suddenly grow pale, as I must have done myself. He let go my wrist, but only to take me in his arms and draw me over to the bed. It has to happen sometime, I was thinking in my confusion, it has to happen. . . .

For this was the round of love: fear which leads on desire, tenderness and fury, and that brutal anguish which triumphantly follows pleasure. I was lucky enough—thanks to Cyril's gentleness—to discover it all that day.

I stayed with him for about an hour. I was happy, but bewildered. I was used to hearing the word love bandied about, and I had often talked about it stupidly myself, as one does when one is young and ignorant. But now I felt I could never talk of love again in that brutal, detached manner.

Cyril, lying beside me, was going on about marrying me and how we would be together always. My silence made him uneasy. I sat up, looked tenderly at him, and murmured: "My lover!" I kissed the vein on his neck, murmuring, "Darling, darling Cyril!"

I was not so sure it was love I felt for him at that moment. I have always been fickle, and I have no wish to delude myself on this point. But just then I loved him more than I loved myself; I would have sacrificed my life for him. When I left him, he asked me if I was angry with him. I just laughed! How could I possibly be angry with him when he had given me such pleasure?

I walked slowly back through the pine woods. I had asked Cyril not to come with me; it would have been too risky. Besides, I was afraid something might show in my face or manner. Anne was lying on a deck chair in front of the house, reading. I had made up a story to explain where I had been. I did not need to use it. She never asked questions. Then I remembered we had quarreled, and I sat down near her in dead silence. I remained motionless, aware of my own breathing and the trembling of my fingers, and thinking of Cyril.

I got a cigarette from the table and struck a match. It went out. With shaking hands I struck another match, and although there was no wind, it, too, went out. In exasperation I took a third, and for some reason this match assumed a vital importance, perhaps because Anne was watching me intently. Suddenly everything around me seemed to melt away and there was nothing left but the match between my fingers, the box, and Anne's eyes boring into me. My heart was beating violently. I tightened my fingers around the match and struck it, but as I bent forward, my cigarette put it out. The matchbox dropped to the ground and I could feel Anne's hard, searching gaze upon me. The tension was unbearable. Then her hands were under my chin, and as she raised my face, I shut my eyes tightly for fear she should read their expression and see the tears welling up, tears of fatigue, of pleasure, of shame. She stroked my cheek, and then let me go, as if she had decided to leave things be. Then she lit a cigarette, put it into my mouth and returned to her book.

Perhaps the incident was symbolic. Sometimes when I am groping for a match, I find myself thinking of that strange moment when my hands no longer seemed to belong to me, and again I recall the intensity of Anne's look, and the emptiness around me—the vast emptiness.

Five

THE INCIDENT I HAVE JUST described was not without its aftermath. Like some self-controlled, self-assured persons, Anne did not like to make compromises. When, on the terrace, she had let me go, she was acting against her principles. She had, of course, guessed something, and it would have been easy enough for her to make me talk. But finally she had yielded to pity or indifference. It was just as hard for her to make allowances for my shortcomings as to try to remove them. In both cases she was prompted merely by a sense of duty. In marrying my father she felt she must also take charge of me. I would have found it easier to accept her constant disapproval if she had sometimes shown exasperation, or any other feeling which went more than skin-deep. One gets used to other people's faults if one does not feel it a duty to correct them.

Within a few months she would have ceased to trouble about me and her indifference might then have been tempered by affection. This attitude would have suited me down to the ground. But it could never happen with her, because her sense of responsibility was too strong, especially since I was still young enough to be influenced. I was malleable, though obstinate.

Therefore she had a feeling of frustration concerning me. She was annoyed with herself and let me see it. A few days later we were at dinner when the controversial subject of my vacation tasks cropped up. I was a bit too offhand, and even my father showed annoyance. But in the end it was Anne who locked me up in my room, although she had not even raised her voice during the argument. I had no idea what she had done until I tried to leave the room to get a glass of water. I had never been locked up, and at first I was in a panic. I rushed over to the window, but there was no escape that way. Then I threw myself against the door so violently that I bruised my shoulder. With my teeth clenched I tried to force the lock with a pair of tweezers. I did not want to call to anyone to open it. After that I stood still in the middle of the room, tried to collect my thoughts, and gradually I became quite calm. This was my first contact with cruelty. I felt it grow in me, as my thoughts gave it substance. I lay stretched out, on my bed, and began to plan my revenge. My ferocity was entirely out of proportion to the cause. In fact several times I went to open the door, and was surprised to find that I could not get out.

At six o'clock my father came to release me. I got up when he came in, and smiled at him. He looked at me in silence.

"Have you anything to say to me as yet?" he asked.

"What about?" I said. "You know we both have a horror of explanations that lead nowhere."

He seemed relieved. "But do try to be nicer to Anne, more patient."

His choice of words surprised me: *me* be patient with Anne? Instead of the other way round. I realized that he thought of Anne as a woman he was imposing on his daughter, instead of the contrary. There was evidently still room for hope.

"I was horrid," I said. "I'll apologize to her."

"You're not unhappy, are you?"

"Of course not!" I replied. "And, anyhow, if she and I quarrel too often, I shall just marry a little earlier, that's all!" I knew my words would strike home.

"You mustn't look at it in that way. You're not Snow White! You wouldn't go away and leave me so soon? We've only had two years together."

The thought was as unbearable for me as for him. I could see myself crying on his shoulder, bewailing our lost happiness. But I would not involve him in my conspiracy.

"You know I always exaggerate. With a few concessions on both sides, Anne and I will get on all right."

"Yes," he said. "Of course!"

He must have thought, as I did at that moment, that the concessions would probably not be mutual, but would be on my side only.

"You see," I told him. "I realize very well that Anne is always right. Her way of living is really far more satisfactory than ours, has greater depth."

He started to protest, but I went on: "In a month or two I shall have completely assimilated Anne's ideas, and there won't be any more stupid arguments between us. It just needs patience."

He was obviously taken aback. He was not only losing a boon companion, but a slice of his past as well.

"Now don't exaggerate again!" he said in a weak voice. "I know that the kind of life you have led with me was perhaps not suitable for your age, or mine either, for that matter, but it was neither dull nor gloomy. After all, we've never been bored or depressed during the last two years, have we? There's no need to be so drastic, just because Anne's conception of life is a little different."

"On the contrary," I said firmly. "We'll have to go even further than I mentioned, give up our old way of life altogether!"

"Oh, I suppose so," said my poor father as we went downstairs together.

I made my apologies to Anne without the slightest

embarrassment. She told me that I needn't have bothered; the heat must have been the cause of our dispute. I felt gay and carefree.

I met Cyril in the pine woods, as we had planned. I told him what to do next. He listened to me with a mixture of fear and admiration. Then he took me in his arms, but I could not stay as it was getting late. I was surprised to find that I did not want to leave him. If he had been searching for the means of attaching me to him, he had certainly found it. My body responded to his and bloomed beside him. I kissed him passionately, I even wanted to bruise him, so that he would not be able to forget me for a single moment all the evening, and would dream of me all night long. I could not bear the thought of the night without him, close to me, without his sudden fury and his long caresses.

Six

THE NEXT MORNING I took my father for a walk along the road. We talked gaily of frivolous matters. I suggested going back to the villa by way of the pine woods. It was exactly half-past ten; just the right time. My father was walking in front of me on the narrow path, pushing aside the brambles so that I should not scratch my legs. When he stopped dead in his tracks I knew he had seen them. I went up to him. There they were, Cyril and Elsa, lying on the pine needles, apparently asleep. Although they were acting entirely on my instructions, and I knew very well that they were not in love, nevertheless they were both young and beautiful, and I could not help feeling a pang of jealousy. I saw that my father was white as a sheet. I took him by the arm.

"Don't let's disturb them. Come on!"

He glanced once more at Elsa, who lay there in all her youthful beauty, all golden, with her red hair and with a half smile on her lips. She seemed indeed a young nymph trapped at last by love. Then he turned on his heel and walked on at a brisk pace. I could hear him muttering: "The bitch! The bitch!"

"Why do you say that? She's free, isn't she?"

"That's not the point! Did you find it very pleasant to see her in Cyril's arms?"

"I don't love him any more," I said.

"Neither do I love Elsa," he answered furiously. "But it hurts just the same. After all, I have . . . ah . . . lived with her. That makes it worse."

Did *I* know that made it worse? Yes, indeed! He must have felt like dashing up to tear them apart and seize his property—or what had once been his property.

"Suppose Anne were to hear you say such a thing!" I said.

"What do you mean? Well, of course she wouldn't understand. She'd be shocked, that's normal enough! But what about you? Don't you understand me any more? Are you shocked, too?"

How easy it was for me to steer his thoughts in the direction I wanted! It was rather frightening to know him so well.

"Of course I'm not shocked," I said. "But you must see things as they are. Elsa has a short memory, she finds Cyril attractive, and that's the end of it as far as you're concerned. After all, look how you behaved to her. It was unforgivable!"

"If I wanted her . . ." my father began and then stopped short.

"You'd have no luck," I said positively, as if it were the most natural thing in the world for me to discuss his chances of getting Elsa back.

"Anyhow it is out of the question," he said in a more resigned voice.

"Of course it is!" I answered with a shrug of my shoulders which was meant to convey that he, poor chap, was out of the running now. He said not another word until we reached the house. Then he took Anne into his arms and held her close to him. She was surprised, but submitted happily to his embrace. I went out of the room, trembling with shame.

At two o'clock, I heard a soft whistle, and went down to join Cyril on the beach. We got into his boat and sailed out to sea. There was nothing in sight; no one else was out in that heat. When we were some way from the shore, he pulled down the sail. So far we had hardly exchanged a word.

"This morning," he began.

"Don't talk," I said. "Oh, please don't talk."

He gently pushed me down in the boat. We were awash, sweaty, awkward and urgent. I could feel the boat swaying as we made love. I watched the sun above me. Suddenly there was the tender, imperious whisper of

Cyril. The sun exploded and fell on me. Where was I? At the bottom of the sea, at the bottom of time, at the bottom of pleasure. I called Cyril in a loud voice. He did not answer. He did not have to answer.

Afterward there was the tang of salt water. We lay in the sun, laughed and were happy. We had the sun and the sea, laughter and love: I wonder if either he or I shall ever again recover the particular brilliance of those days. And for me they were heightened by an undercurrent of anxiety and remorse.

I found, beyond the very real physical pleasure of love, a kind of intellectual pleasure in thinking about it. The words "to make," material and positive, united with the poetical abstraction of the word "love," enchanted me. I had said them before without the least embarrassment or without noticing their special savor. Now I found myself prudish. I lowered my gaze when my father turned his eyes to Anne as she laughed her low laugh, indecently intimate, which made us pale, my father and me, and look out of the window. Had we told Anne that her laugh revealed her so, she would not have believed us. She did not act like a mistress with my father, but like a friend, a tender friend. But in the night . . . I turned from such thoughts, I hated such disturbing ideas.

The time passed quickly. I almost forgot Anne, my father, and Elsa. Through love I had entered another world. I felt dreamy, yet wide awake, peaceful and contented. Cyril asked me if I were not afraid of having a child. I told him that I was entirely in his hands, and he seemed satisfied that it should be so. Perhaps I had given myself to him because I knew that if I had a child, he would be prepared to take the blame. He was ready to take on what I could never face: responsibility. Besides, I could not imagine myself pregnant, with my slight, hard body. . . . For once I was thankful for my adolescent figure.

But Elsa was growing impatient. She plied me with questions. I was always afraid of being seen with her or Cyril. She lay in wait for my father at every likely spot, and tried to convince herself that he had difficulty in keeping away from her. I was surprised that this woman of pleasure, who had always associated love with money, should get such romantic ideas, be excited by a look or a gesture, when such things had usually been merely routine for her. The role she was playing evidently seemed to her the height of psychological subtlety.

Though my father was gradually becoming obsessed with the thought of Elsa, Anne did not seem to notice it. He was more affectionate and demonstrative than ever with her, which frightened me, because I attributed it to his subconscious guilt. In three weeks we should be back in Paris, and the main thing was that nothing should happen before then. Elsa would be out of our way, and my father and Anne would get married if by then they had not changed their minds. In Paris I would have Cyril, and just as Anne had been unable to keep us apart here, so she would find it impossible to stop me from seeing him once we were home. In Paris, Cyril had a room away from his mother. I could already imagine the window open to the pink and blue sky, the wonderful sky of Paris, with the pigeons cooing on the window sill, and with Cyril beside me on the narrow bed. . . .

Seven

A FEW DAYS LATER my father received a message from one of our friends asking us to meet him at a café in Saint Raphael for a drink. He was pleased at the thought of escaping for a while from this unusual seclusion in which we had chosen to live. He could hardly wait to tell us the news. I mentioned to Elsa and Cyril that we would be at the Bar du Soleil at seven o'clock and if they liked to come, they would see us there. Then I learned that Elsa happened to know the friend we were meeting, which made her all the more keen to go. So I realized that there might be complications, and tried in vain to put her off.

"Charles Webb simply adores me," she said, with childlike simplicity. "If he sees me, his response is sure to make Raymond want to come back to me."

Cyril did not care whether he went to Saint Raphael or

not. I saw by the way he looked at me that he wanted only to be near me, and I felt proud.

At six o'clock we drove off in Anne's car. It was a huge American convertible, which she kept more for publicity than to suit her own taste, but it suited mine down to the ground, with all its shiny gadgets. Another advantage was that we could all three sit in front, and I never felt so happy as when I was in a car with the two of them, elbow to elbow, sharing the same pleasures, and perhaps even the same death. Anne was at the wheel, as if symbolizing her future place in the family. This was the first time I had been in her car since the evening we went to Cannes.

We met Charles Webb and his wife at the Bar du Soleil. He was engaged in theatrical publicity; his wife spent all his earnings on entertaining young men. Money was an obsession with him. He thought of nothing else in his unceasing effort to make ends meet; hence his restless impatience. He had been Elsa's lover for a long time, and she had suited him quite well, because, though very pretty, she was not particularly grasping.

His wife was a malicious woman. Anne had never met her, and I noticed that Anne's lovely face quickly assumed the superior, mocking expression that was habitual with her in society. As usual Charles Webb talked all the time, now and then giving Anne an inquisitive look. He evidently wondered how Anne came to be with that notorious lady-killer, Raymond, and his daughter. I was glad to think he would soon find out. Just then my father leaned forward and said abruptly:

"I have news for you, old chap. Anne and I are getting married on the fifth of October."

Webb looked from one to the other in amazement. His wife, who had rather a weakness for my father, seemed disconcerted.

After a pause, Webb shouted: "Congratulations! What a splendid idea! My dear lady, you don't know what you're taking on! You are wonderful! Here, waiter! We must celebrate!"

Anne smiled quietly and calmly. Then I saw Webb's face light up; I had no need to turn around.

"Elsa! Good heavens! It's Elsa Mackenbourg! She hasn't noticed me yet. I say, Raymond, do you see how lovely that girl has grown?"

"Hasn't she?" said my father in a proprietary tone, but then he remembered, and his face fell.

Anne could hardly help noticing that inflection in his voice. She turned to me with a quick movement, but before she could speak I leaned toward her and said in a confidential whisper, loud enough for my father to hear:

"Anne, you're causing quite a sensation. There's a man over there who can't take his eyes off you."

My father twisted around to look at the man in question.

"I won't tolerate that sort of thing!" he said, taking Anne's hand.

"Aren't they sweet?" exclaimed Mrs. Webb, ironically. "Charles, we really shouldn't have disturbed them. It would have been better to have invited little Cécile all by herself."

"Little Cécile wouldn't have come," I said unhesitatingly.

"Why not? Are you in love with one of the fishermen?"

Mrs. Webb had once seen me in conversation with a bus conductor, and ever since had treated me as though I had lost caste.

"Why yes, of course!" I said with an effort to appear gay.

"And do you go out fishing a lot with him?"

She thought she was being witty, which made it worse. I was beginning to get angry.

"I don't specialize in mackerel," I said. "But I do go fishing."

There was a dead silence. They evidently understood my pun. Anne's voice interposed quietly:

"Raymond, would you mind asking the waiter to bring me a straw to drink my orange juice?"

Charles Webb began to talk feverishly about having another round of drinks. I could see from the way my father was staring into his glass that he was longing to laugh. Anne gave me a look of entreaty. Nevertheless we all decided to dine together, just to show there were no hard feelings.

At dinner I drank too much. I wanted to forget Anne's anxious expression when she looked at my father, and the hint of gratitude in her eyes whenever they rested on me. Every time Mrs. Webb made a dig at me I answered it with an ingratiating smile. This seemed to upset her, and she soon became openly aggressive. Anne signed to me to keep quiet. She had a horror of scenes in public, and Mrs. Webb was on the verge of creating one. For my part, I was used to them. Among our associates, they were frequent, so I was not disturbed by the prospect.

After dinner we went to another bar. Soon Elsa and Cyril turned up. Elsa was talking very loud as she entered the room followed by poor Cyril. I thought she was behaving badly, but she was pretty enough to carry it off.

"Who's that puppy she's with?" asked Charles Webb. "He's rather young, isn't he?"

"It's love that keeps him young!" simpered his wife.

"Don't you believe it!" said my father. "She's not in love with him. He's just a passing fancy."

I had my eyes on Anne. She was watching Elsa in the calm, detached way she looked at very young women, or at the mannequins who exhibited her creations. For a moment I admired her tremendously for showing no trace of jealousy or spite. But how could she be jealous, I wondered, when she herself was a hundred times more beautiful and intelligent than Elsa? As I was very drunk, I told her so. She looked at me curiously.

"Do you really think I am more beautiful than Elsa?"

"Of course!"

"That is always pleasant to hear. But you are drinking too much again. Give me your drink. I hope it doesn't upset you to see Cyril here. Anyway, he seems bored to death."

"He's my lover," I said with gay abandon.

"You *are* quite drunk! Thank goodness, it's time to go home."

It was a relief to part from the Webbs. I found it difficult to say good-by politely. My father drove the car, and my head lolled onto Anne's shoulder.

I was thinking how much I preferred her to the people we usually saw, how infinitely superior she was in every way. My father said very little; perhaps he was thinking of Elsa.

"Is she sleeping?" he asked Anne.

"As peaceful as a baby. She didn't behave badly on the whole, did she? Of course she should not have made that remark about mackerel."

My father laughed. They were silent for a while, then I heard his voice again:

"Anne, I love you, only you. Do you believe me?"

"Don't tell me so often. It frightens me."

"Give me your hand."

I almost sat up to protest: "For heaven's sake, not on the Corniche!" But I was too drunk, and still half asleep. Besides, there was Anne's perfume, the sea breeze in my hair, the little scratch on my shoulder was a reminder of

Cyril's love making, all these reasons to be happy and keep quiet. I thought of Elsa and Cyril setting off on the motorcycle which had been a birthday present from his mother. I felt so sorry for them that I almost cried. Anne's car was made for sleeping. It rode so gently, not noisy like a motorcycle. I thought of Mrs. Webb lying awake at night. No doubt at her age I would also have to pay someone to love me, because love is the most wonderful thing in the world. Love was worth whatever it cost. The important thing was not to become embittered and jealous, as she was of Elsa and Anne. I began to laugh softly to myself. Anne shifted her shoulder to make a comfortable hollow for me.

"Go to sleep," she ordered.

I went to sleep.

Eight

THE NEXT MORNING I woke up feeling perfectly well except for a slight ache in my neck. My bed was flooded with sunshine as it was every morning. I threw back the sheets and exposed my bare back to the sun. It was warm and comforting, and seemed to penetrate my very bones. I decided to spend the morning like that, without moving.

In my mind I went over the events of the evening before. I remembered telling Anne that Cyril was my lover. It amused me to think that if one told the truth when drunk, nobody believed it. I thought about Mrs. Webb. I was used to that sort of woman; in circles like hers and at her age they often become unpleasant through lack of enough opportunities to indulge themselves. Anne's calm dignity had shown Mrs. Webb up as even more idiotic and boring than usual. It was only to be expected. I could not imagine anyone among my father's old friends who could for a moment bear comparison with Anne. In order to be able to face an evening with people like that, one had either to be rather drunk and enjoy quarreling with them, or else be on intimate terms with one or other of the group. For my father it was easy: Charles Webb and he were both libertines. "Guess who is dining and sleeping with me tonight? The little Mars girl, in Saurel's latest film. I was going into Dupuis' house and . . ." then my father would laugh and tap him on the shoulder.

"Lucky man! She's almost as pretty as Elsa."

Undergraduate talk, but I liked their liveliness. Then there were interminable evenings on café terraces, and Lombard's tales of woe. "She was the only one I ever really loved, Raymond! Do you remember that spring, before she left me?" "It is stupid for a man to devote his whole life to one woman." All this touched on the indecent, this embarrassing but hot-blooded talk of two men who told "all" over a drink.

Anne's friends probably never talked about themselves. Perhaps they did not indulge in such adventures. Or if they spoke of them at all, it would be with an apologetic laugh. Already I almost shared Anne's condescending attitude toward our friends; it was catching. On the other hand, by the age of thirty, I could imagine myself being more like them than like Anne, and then her silence, her detachment and her reserve might suffocate me. In fifteen years, a little blasé, I would lean seductively to an equally world-weary man and say:

"My first lover was called Cyril. I was almost eighteen, it was hot by the sea. . . ."

I imagined the man's face. He would have little wrinkles like my father.

There was a knock at the door. I quickly put on my pajama top and called, "Come in!" Anne stood there, carefully holding a cup.

"I thought you might like some coffee. How do you feel this morning?"

"Very well," I answered. "I'm afraid I was a bit tipsy last night."

"As you are each time you go out!" She began to laugh. "But I must say, you were amusing. It was such a tedious evening."

I had forgotten the sun, and even my coffee. When I was talking to Anne, I was completely absorbed. I did not think of myself, and yet she was the only one who made me question my motives. Through her I lived more intensely.

"Cécile, do you really find people like the Webbs and the Dupuis entertaining?"

"Well, they usually behave abominably, but they *are* funny."

She was watching a fly on the floor. Anne's eyelids were long and heavy; it was easy for her to look condescending.

"Don't you ever realize how monotonous and dull their conversation is? Don't those endless stories about girls, business contracts and drinking parties bore you?"

"I'm afraid," I answered, "that after ten years of convent life their lack of morals fascinates me."

I did not dare to add that I also liked it.

"For two years?" she said. "It's not a question of reason, however, or of morals. It is a question of one's sensibility, a sixth sense."

I supposed I didn't have it. I saw clearly that I was lacking in this respect.

"Anne," I asked abruptly, "do you think I am intelligent?"

She began to laugh, surprised at the directness of my question.

"Of course you are! Why do you ask?"

"If I were an idiot, you'd say just the same thing," I sighed. "I so often find your superiority overpowering."

"It's just a question of age," she answered. "It would be a sad thing if I didn't have a little more self-assurance than you or *you* would dominate *me*!"

She laughed, but I was annoyed.

"That wouldn't necessarily be a bad thing."

"It would be a catastrophe," she said quietly.

She suddenly stopped her bantering tone and looked me straight in the face. I at once felt ill at ease, and began to fidget. Even today I cannot get used to people who stare at me, while they are talking, or come very close to make sure that I am listening. My only thought is to escape. I go on saying "Yes" while gradually edging away. Their insistence and pertinacity enrage me. What right have they to try to corner me? Fortunately Anne did not resort to all these tactics, but she did keep her eyes fixed on me, so that I could no longer talk in the lighthearted vein I usually affected.

"Do you realize how men like Webb end up?" she said.

I thought, "And men like my father."

"In the river," I answered flippantly.

"A time comes when they are no longer attractive or in good form. They can't drink any more, and they still hanker after women. Only then they have to pay heavily and lower their standards, to escape from their loneliness. Then they are really laughingstocks. They grow sentimental and querulous. I have seen many who have gone that way."

"Poor Webb!" I said.

I was impressed. So that was the fate in store for my father? Or at least the fate from which Anne was saving him.

"You never thought of that, did you?" said Anne, with a little smile of commiseration. "You don't think much about the future, do you? But that is the privilege of youth."

"Please don't throw my youth at me like that! I use it neither as an excuse, nor as a privilege. I just don't attach any importance to it."

"To what *do* you attach importance? To your peace of mind? Your freedom?"

I dreaded conversations of this sort, especially with Anne.

"To nothing at all," I said. "You know very well I hardly ever think."

"You and your father irritate me at times. You haven't given it a thought. You're not good for anything. You don't know. Are you really content to be like that?"

"I'm not content with myself. I don't like myself, and I don't try to. At moments you force me to complicate my life, and I hold it against you."

She began to hum to herself, with a thoughtful expression. I recognized the tune, but did not know what it was.

"What's the name of that song, Anne? It gets on my nerves."

"I don't know," she smiled again, looking rather discouraged. "Stay in bed and rest. I'll continue my research on the family intellect somewhere else."

I thought it was easy enough for my father to get out of it. I could just imagine his saying, "I'm not thinking of anything except that I love you, Anne." In spite of her intelligence, Anne would accept this as a valid excuse. I indulged myself in a good stretch and pushed my head deep into my pillow. Anne was dramatizing the situation, I thought. In twenty-five years my father would be an amiable man of sixty-five with white hair, rather addicted to whisky and high-colored reminiscences. We would go out together; it would be my turn to tell him *my* adventures, and his to advise me. I realized that in my mind I was excluding Anne from our future; I did not see how she could fit in.

In the turmoil of our disorderly Paris flat, sometimes forlorn, at others full of flowers, the stage of many and varied scenes, often cluttered up with luggage, I somehow could not envisage the introduction of order, the peace and quiet, the feeling of harmony that Anne brought with her everywhere, as if they were the most precious of gifts. I dreaded being bored to death. But I was less apprehensive of her influence since my love affair with Cyril, which had liberated me from many of my anxieties. Still, I feared boredom and tranquillity more than anything else. In order to achieve inner peace, my father and I had to have excitement. And this Anne was not prepared to admit.

Nine

I HAVE SPOKEN a great deal about Anne and myself, and very little of my father. Yet he has played the most important part in this story, and my feelings for him have been deeper and more stable than for anyone else. I know him too well, and feel too close to him to talk easily of him, and it is he above all others whom I wish to justify and present in a good light. He was neither vain nor selfish, but just incurably frivolous. I could not call him irresponsible or incapable of deep feelings. His love for me is not to be taken lightly, or regarded merely as a parental habit. He could suffer more through me than through anyone else, and, for my part, I was nearer to despair the day he turned away as if abandoning me, than I had ever been in my life. I was always more important to him than his love affairs. On many evenings, by taking me home from parties, he must have often missed what his friend Webb would have called "a fine chance." On the other hand, I cannot deny that he was inconstant and would always take the easiest way. He never meditated. He tried to give everything a physiological explanation, which he called being rational. "You don't like yourself as you are? Just sleep a little more and drink a little less!" It was the same when at times he had a violent desire for a particular woman. He never thought of repressing it, or trying to elevate it into a deeper sentiment. He was a materialist, if kind and understanding, with a touch of delicacy. His desire for Elsa disturbed him, though not in the way one might expect. He did not say to himself: "I want to be unfaithful to Anne, therefore I must love her less," but: "This need for Elsa is a nuisance. I must get over it quickly or it might cause complications with Anne." Moreover he loved and admired Anne. She was a change from the stupid, frivolous women he had known in recent years. She satisfied his vanity, his sensuality and his sensibility all at once, for she understood him. She offered her intelligence and experience to supplement his. Yet I do not believe he realized how deeply she cared for him. He thought of her as the ideal mistress, the ideal mother for me, however I do not think he visualized her as the ideal wife for himself—with all the obligations this would entail. I am sure that in Cyril's and in Anne's eyes he was, like me, abnormal, so to speak. Still the fact that he had no high regard for his way of living did not prevent him from making it exciting or putting all his vitality into it.

I was not really concerned about him when I formed the project of shutting Anne out of our lives; I knew he would console himself with someone else, as he always had. A clean break with Anne would in the long run be less painful than living a well-regulated life as her husband. What really would destroy him, as it would me, was being subjected to fixed habits. We were of the same race. Sometimes I thought we belonged to a pure and beautiful race of nomads, and at others to a poor, withered breed of sensualists.

At that moment he was suffering, or at least he was feeling exasperated. Elsa had become the symbol of youth and his recent gay life, above all of his own youth. I knew he was dying to say to Anne:

"Dearest, let me go for just one day. I must prove to myself, with Elsa's help, that I'm not an old fogey."

Now that was impossible, not because Anne was jealous, or too virtuous to discuss such matters, but because she had made up her mind to live with him on her own terms. She was determined to put an end to the era of frivolity and debauchery and to stop his schoolboy behavior. She was entrusting her life to him and in the future he must behave well and not be a slave to his caprices. One could not blame Anne; hers was a perfectly normal and sane point of view. Yet it did not keep my father from wanting Elsa, from desiring her more and more as time passed and she was still unobtainable.

At that moment I have no doubt that I could have arranged everything. I had only to tell Elsa to meet him and let him have a quick fling. I could easily have persuaded Anne to go with me to Nice for a whole afternoon on some pretext. On our return we would have found my father relaxed, and filled with a new appreciation of legalized affection, or, rather, affection shortly to become legalized. But Anne could not have borne the idea of having been a mistress like the others. How difficult she made life for us through her dignity and self-respect.

But I said nothing to Elsa, neither did I ask Anne to go to Nice with me. I wanted my father's desire to fester in him, so that in the end he would give himself away. I could not bear the contempt with which Anne treated our past life, her disdain for what had been our happiness. I had no wish to humiliate her, but only to force her to accept our way of life. For this it was necessary that she should discover my father's infidelity, should see it objectively as a physical indulgence, not as an attack on her personal dignity. If at all costs she wanted to be right, she must allow us to be wrong.

I even pretended not to notice my father's plight. On no account would I become his intermediary by speaking to Elsa for him, or getting Anne out of the way. I had to pretend to look upon Anne and his love for her as sacred, and I must admit it was not difficult for me. The idea that he could be unfaithful and defy her filled me with terror and a vague awe.

Meanwhile we had many happy days. I made use of every occasion to further my father's interest in Elsa. The sight of Anne's face no longer filled me with remorse. I sometimes imagined that she would accept everything, and that we would be able to live a life that suited us all three equally well. I saw Cyril often. We made love in secret and I was under the spell of the scent of pines, the sound of the sea, and the contact of his body. . . .

Cyril began to torment himself. He hated the role I had forced upon him, and continued in it only because I made him believe it was necessary for our love. All this involved a great deal of deceit, and much had to be concealed. But it did not cost me much effort to tell a few lies, and after all, I alone was in control, was the sole judge of my actions.

I will pass quickly over this period, for I am afraid that if I look at it closely, I shall revive memories that are too painful. Even now I feel overwhelmed as I think of Anne's happy laugh, of her kindness to me. My conscience troubles me so much at these moments that I am obliged to resort to some expedient like lighting a cigarette, putting on a record, or telephoning to a friend. Then gradually I begin to think of something else. But I do not like having to take refuge in forgetfulness and frivolity instead of facing my memories and fighting them.

Ten

FATE SOMETIMES ASSUMES strange forms. And that summer it appeared in the guise of Elsa, a mediocre person, although attractive. She had an extraordinary laugh, sudden and infectious, the kind that only rather stupid people possess.

I had soon noticed the effect of this laugh on my father. I told her to make the utmost use of it whenever we "surprised" her with Cyril. My orders were: "When you hear me coming with my father, say nothing, just laugh." And at the sound of that laugh a look of fury would come into my father's face. My role of stage manager continued to be exciting. I never missed my mark, for when we saw Cyril and Elsa openly showing signs of their imaginary relationship, my father and I both grew pale with the intensity of our feelings. The sight of Cyril bending over Elsa made my heart ache. I would have given anything in the world to stop them, forgetting for the moment that it was I who had planned it.

Apart from these incidents, our daily life was filled with Anne's confidence, gentleness, and (I hate to use the word) her happiness. She was nearer to happiness than I had ever seen her since she had been with us, egotists that we were. She was far removed from our violent desires and my base little schemes. I counted on her aloofness and instinctive pride to keep her from using any special effort to hold my father to her, counted on her relying only on her beauty, her intelligence, her own loving self. I began to feel sorry for her, and pity is an agreeable sentiment, uplifting like military music.

One fine morning the maid, visibly worked up, handed me a note from Elsa:

"All goes well. Come!"

I had a feeling of imminent catastrophe. I hate theatrical denouements. I met Elsa on the beach; she was looking triumphant.

"I have just been talking to your father, just an hour ago."

"What did he say?"

"He told me he was very sorry for what had happened, that he had behaved like a cad. That's the truth, isn't it?"

I thought it best to agree.

"Then he paid me compliments in the way only he can, you know, quietly, in a low voice, as if at the same time he was suffering."

I interrupted her.

"What was he leading up to?"

"Well, nothing. . . . Oh yes, he asked me to have tea with him in the village to show I had no ill-feeling, and that I was forgiving. Shall I go?"

My father's views on the need for forgiving natures in red-headed girls were a treat to hear. I came near saying that it didn't matter to me. Then I realized that she credited me with this success. Nevertheless, it irritated me. I felt trapped.

"I don't know, Elsa. That depends on you. You always ask me what you should do. One might almost believe that it was I who induced you . . ."

"But it was you," she said. "It's entirely through you that . . ."

The admiration in her voice suddenly frightened me.

"Go if you want to, but for heaven's sake, don't talk any more about it!"

"But, Cécile, isn't the whole idea to free him from that woman's clutches?"

I fled. Let my father do as he wished, and Anne must deal with it as best she could. Anyhow, I was on my way to meet Cyril. It seemed to me that love was the only remedy for the haunting anxiety I felt.

Cyril took me in his arms. Without a word he led me away. With him everything became easy, charged as it was with ardor and with pleasure. Later, stretched out beside his sunburned body, bathed in perspiration, I was drained of feeling, lost like a shipwrecked soul, and I told him that I hated myself. I smiled as I said it because, although I meant it, there was no pain, only an enjoyable resignation. He did not take me seriously.

"Never mind. I love you so much that I shall make you feel about yourself as I do."

All through our midday meal, I thought of his words: "I love you so much." That is why, although I have tried hard, I cannot remember much about that lunch. Anne was wearing a mauve dress, as mauve as the shadows under her eyes, the color of her eyes themselves. My father laughed a lot, and was evidently well pleased with himself. Everything was going well for him. During dessert he announced that he had some shopping to do in the village that afternoon. I smiled to myself. I was tired of the whole thing, and felt fatalistic about it. My one desire was to have a swim.

At four o'clock I went down to the beach. I saw my father on the terrace about to leave for the village; I did not speak to him, not even to warn him to be cautious.

The water was soft and warm. Anne did not appear. I supposed she was busy in her room designing her next collection. Meanwhile my father would be making the most of his time with Elsa. After two hours, when I was tired of sunbathing, I went up to our terrace, and, sitting down in a chair, opened a newspaper.

At that moment Anne appeared from the direction of the woods. She was running, clumsily, heavily, her elbows close to her sides. I had a sudden, ghastly impression of an old woman running toward me, that she was about to fall down. I did not move; she disappeared behind the house, going toward the garage. In a flash I understood and I, too, began running, to catch her.

She was already in her car starting it up. I rushed over and clutched at the door.

"Anne," I cried, "Don't go. It's all a mistake! It's my fault. I'll explain everything!"

She paid no attention to me, but bent to release the brake.

"Anne, we need you!"

She straightened up, and I saw that her face was distorted. She was crying. For the first time I realized that I had hurt a living, sensitive creature, not just a personality. She, too, must once have been a rather secretive small girl, later on an adolescent, and after that a woman. . . . Now she was forty, and all alone. She loved a man, and had hoped to spend ten or twenty happy years with him. As for me . . . that poor miserable face was my doing.

I was petrified. I trembled all over as I leaned against the car door.

"You have no need of anyone," she murmured. "Neither you nor he."

The engine was running. I was desperate; she mustn't go like that!

"Forgive me! I beg you . . ."

"Forgive you! What for?"

The tears were streaming down her face. She did not seem to notice them.

"My poor child!" she said.

She laid her hand against my cheek for a moment then drove off. I saw her car disappearing around the side of the house. I was irretrievably lost. It had all happened so quickly. I thought again of her face.

I heard steps behind me. It was my father. He had taken the time to remove the imprint of Elsa's lipstick from his face and brush the pine needles from his suit. I turned around and threw myself on him.

"You beast!"

Then I began to sob.

"But what's the matter? Where is Anne? Cécile, tell me! Cécile!"

Eleven

MY FATHER AND I did not see each other again until dinner time. Both of us were nervous at being suddenly alone together, and neither he nor I had any appetite. We realized we had to get Anne back. I could not bear to think of the look of horror on her face before she left, of her suffering, and my responsibility for it. All my cunning maneuvers and carefully laid plans were forgotten. I was thrown completely off balance, and I could see from his expression that my father felt the same way.

"Do you think," he said, "that she'll stay away from us for long?"

"I expect she's gone back to Paris," I said.

"Paris!" murmured my father in a dreamy voice.

"Perhaps we shall never see her again," I said gloomily.

He seemed at a loss for words, and took my hand across the table.

"You must be terribly angry with me. I don't know what came over me. I was walking back through the woods with Elsa . . . and I . . . ah . . . kissed her, and just at that moment Anne must have come along."

I was not listening. The forms of Elsa and my father embracing under the pines seemed theatrical and unreal to me, and I could not visualize them. The only vivid memory of that day was my last glimpse of Anne's face with its look of grief and betrayal. I took a cigarette from my father's pack and lit it. Smoking during meals was a thing Anne could not bear.

I smiled at my father. "I understand very well. It's not your fault. It was a momentary lapse, as they say. But we must get Anne to forgive us, or rather forgive *you*."

"What shall we do?" he asked me.

He looked far from well. I felt sorry for him and for myself, too. After all, why should Anne act like this, leave us in the lurch, make us suffer so for one little moment of folly?

Hadn't she a duty toward us?

"Let's write to her," I said finally. "Ask her to forgive us."

At last he had found some means of escape from the stupor and remorse of the past three hours. Without waiting to finish our meal, we turned back the tablecloth.

My father went to get a lamp, pens and some notepaper. We sat down opposite each other, almost smiling because our preparations had made Anne's return seem probable. A bat was circling around outside the window. My father started writing.

An unbearable feeling of disgust and horror rises in me when I think of the letters full of fine sentiments we wrote that evening, sitting under the lamp like two awkward schoolchildren, applying ourselves in silence to the impossible task of getting Anne back. However, we managed to produce two works of art, full of excuses, love and repentance. When I had finished mine, I felt almost certain that Anne would not be able to resist us, and that a reconciliation was imminent. I could already imagine the scene as she forgave us. It would take place in our drawing room in Paris. Anne would come in and. . . .

At that moment the telephone rang. It was ten o'clock. We exchanged a look of astonishment which soon turned to hope. It must be Anne telephoning to say she forgave us and would return. My father bounded to the telephone and called: "Hello!" in a voice full of joy.

Then he said nothing but: "Yes, yes! Where is that? Yes!" in an almost inaudible whisper. I got up, shaken by fear. My father passed his hand over his face automatically. At length he slowly replaced the receiver and turned to me.

"She has had an accident," he said. "On the road to

Esterel. It took them some time to discover her address. They telephoned to Paris and got our number from there."

He went on in the same flat voice, and I dared not interrupt.

"The accident happened at the most dangerous spot. There have been many at that place, it seems. The car rolled down the bluff for about one hundred fifty feet. It would have been a miracle if she had survived."

The rest of the night I remember only as one remembers a nightmare: the road surging up under the headlights, my father's stony face, the entrance to the hospital. My father would not let me see her. I sat on a bench in the waiting room looking at a lithograph of Venice. My mind was a blank. A nurse told me that this was the sixth accident at that spot since the beginning of the summer. It was a long time before my father came back to me.

Then it occurred to me that even in her death, Anne had once more proved how different she was from us. If we had wanted to commit suicide, even supposing we had the courage, it would have been with a bullet in the head, with an explanatory note intended to trouble the sleep of those who had led us to the act. But Anne had made us the magnificent present of allowing us to believe it an accident. A dangerous spot on the road, a car that easily lost balance. It was a gift that we would soon be weak enough to accept. In any case it is a romantic idea of mine to call it suicide. Can one commit suicide on account of people like my father and myself, people who have no need of anybody, living or dead? My father and I never spoke of it to each other as anything but an accident.

The next day we returned to the house at about three o'clock in the afternoon. Elsa and Cyril were waiting for us, sitting on the steps. They seemed like two comic, forgotten characters in the drama. Neither of them had known Anne, or loved her. There they were with their little love affairs, their good looks and their embarrassment. Cyril came up to me and put his hand on my arm. I looked at him: I had never loved him! I had found him sweet and attractive. I had loved the pleasure he gave me, but I did not need him. I was going away, leaving behind me the villa, the garden and that summer. My father was beside me. He took my arm and we went indoors.

In the house were Anne's jacket, her flowers, her room, her scent. My father closed the shutters, took a bottle out of the refrigerator and brought two glasses. It was the only remedy at hand. Our letters of excuse still lay on the table. I pushed them off and they floated to the floor. My father, who was coming toward me holding a full glass, hesitated, then avoided them. I found it symbolical. I took my glass and drained it in one gulp. The room was in half-darkness. I saw my father's shadow on the window. The sea was still beating rhythmically on the shore.

Twelve

THE FUNERAL TOOK PLACE in Paris on a fine day. There was the usual crowd of the curious dressed in black. My father and I shook hands with Anne's elderly relations. I looked at them with interest; they would probably have come to tea with us once a year. People cast pitying glances at my father. Webb must have spread the news of his intended marriage. I saw that Cyril was looking for me after the service, but I avoided him. The resentment I felt toward him was quite unjustified, but I could not help it. Everyone was deploring the dreadful, senseless accident, and, as I was still rather doubtful whether it had been an accident, I was relieved.

In the car on the way home, my father took my hand and held it tightly. I thought: "Now we have only each other. We are alone and unhappy." For the first time I cried. My tears were some comfort. They were not at all like the terrible emptiness I had felt in the hospital in front of the picture of Venice. My father gave me his handkerchief without a word. His face was ravaged.

For a month we lived like a widower and an orphan, eating all our meals together and staying at home. Sometimes we spoke of Anne. "Do you remember the day when . . ." We chose our words with care, and averted our eyes for fear we might hurt each other, or that something irreparable would come between us. Our discretion and restraint brought their own recompense. Soon we could speak of Anne in a normal way as of a person dear to us, with whom we could have been happy, but whom God had called to Himself. I have written God, and not fate—but we did not believe in God. In these circumstances we were thankful to believe in fate.

Then one day at a friend's house I met a cousin of hers and liked him and he liked me. For a week I went out with him constantly, and my father, who could not bear to be alone, followed my example with a rather ambitious young woman. Life began to take its old course, as it was bound to. Now, when my father and I are alone together, we joke and discuss our latest conquests. He must suspect that my friendship with Philippe is not platonic, and I know very well that his new friend is costing him too much money. But we are happy. Winter is drawing to an end. We shall not rent the same villa again, but another one, near Juan-les-Pins.

Only when I am in bed, at dawn, listening to the cars

passing below in the streets of Paris, my memory betrays me. That summer returns to me with all its memories. Anne, Anne, I repeat over and over again softly in the darkness. Something rises in me that I call to by name, with closed eyes. *Bonjour, tristesse!*

Insights, Interviews & More . . .

About the author

About the book

Read on

About the author

Born Françoise Quoirez on June 21, 1935, in Cajarc, France, Françoise Sagan was only eighteen when her first novel, *Bonjour Tristesse* (based on her own experiences), was published. Sagan was one of the first celebrity writers for *Cosmopolitan* in the seventies and is known to have lived quite a scandalous life in France, forming the group "La bande Sagan" with Juliette Gréco. Sagan is also the author of *Incidental Music, A Certain Smile, A Fleeting Sorrow, Lost Profile,* and *The Painted Lady*, all out of print in the United States.

What the Papers Said

"With her death, France loses one of its most brilliant and most sensitive writers—an eminent figure of our literary life." —President Jacques Chirac, *Herald* (Glasgow), September 2004

The Beginning

"Sagan was born Françoise Quoirez to Pierre and Marie Quoirez in Carjac, a small town east of Bordeaux. The youngest of three children of an upper-middle-class Catholic family, Sagan was headstrong and fearless." —*Herald Sun* (Melbourne, Australia), September 2004

The Student

"She grew up in sheltered luxury on a country estate near Lyons, but, a spoiled child, did willfully badly at her expensive schools. While dutifully failing to study at the Sorbonne, she fell gradually in with various proponents of what was then the fashionable philosophy—existentialism. She failed her second-year exams and decided to write a novel."

—*Times* (London), September 2004

"She skipped lectures to sit in pavement cafés and watched the passing show on the boulevards—especially the young men, and indeed some of the older roués who were still presentable. At every opportunity she attended the popular concerts of American jazz at the Vieux Colombier, and danced to Sidney Bechet. Then there would be a mad dash across Paris to be home in time for dinner." —*Independent* (London), September 2004

The *Enfant Terrible*

"Sagan retained her ability to shock. An early headline in the *Daily Sketch* demanded 'Does she know too much about sex?' She was denounced by the Pope. But her aura of glamour and insouciance was backed up by strength in the face of tragedy, and she believed in living hard and without complaint, like her idol Billie Holiday."

—*Financial Times* (London), September 2004

"She set about blowing the money [from sales of *Bonjour Tristesse*], and her antics behind the wheel and at the gaming tables, as well as her meetings with figures such as Truman Capote and Tennessee Williams, were by turns condemned as gross immorality and lauded as signals of emancipation." —*Australian*, September 2004

"Sagan was not shy in presenting to her public a version of the responsibility-free lifestyle endorsed in her work. She would leave her sports cars haphazardly in the road outside the doors of nightclubs, breakfast on Gauloises and coffee, and play to lurid rumors of her sex life. Her entourage came to be known as the pinnacle of youthful sophistication." —*Times* (London), September 2004

"[F]ollowing [Sagan's] conviction for drug abuse, the radical right-wing politician Jean-Marie Le Pen petitioned for her to be guillotined. It is even rumored that he asked the French Ministry of the Interior to have her banned from casinos." —*Moscow News*, September 2004

"[A] parish priest refused to officiate at her first wedding because of her books, which he considered immoral." —*Washington Post*, September 2004

"A longtime smoker with a penchant for fast cars, Sagan was fined for using cocaine in the mid-1990s and ordered to seek treatment. In 2002, a court convicted her of tax fraud." —*Variety*, October 2004

The Driver

"Upon receiving payment for *Bonjour Tristesse* . . . Sagan immediately purchased a sports car and made a dash for St. Tropez. This was the beginning of a nonstop, self-destructive lifestyle, indulged with a generous dose of hedonistic revelry at every curve. One such curve happened in 1957 when she failed to negotiate a bend in her Aston Martin. The accident left her in a coma for three days." —*Moscow News*, September 2004

"The huge success of this first novel allowed her to purchase her first Jaguar XK 140—second-hand but a real treasure for Sagan, whose love ▶

What the Papers Said *(continued)*

of speed was to involve her in a series of near-fatal accidents requiring painful surgery, which led her to depend more and more on painkilling drugs to which she added shots of whiskey, another demon that was to haunt her life." —*Independent* (London), September 2004

"France may cherish some rather outdated illusions about the British gentleman driver. But, it seems, it still has some way to go before it rids itself of the kind of attitude summed up by the late Françoise Sagan, who was once given the last rites after a car crash.

" 'You can always die getting hit on the head by a flower pot,' Sagan said. 'But to die suddenly in a fast car—for a Frenchman, that's a fabulous death.' " —*Guardian* (London), March 2005

The Writer

"While critics condemned her for writing only about the rich, she maintained they were all she knew.

" 'It is out of the question for me to describe the love affair between a junk man and a factory girl,' she once said. 'It would be bad form for me to describe people I don't know and don't understand.' " —*Courier Mail* (Queensland, Australia), September 2004

"A prolific worker, she went on to produce other resonant titles—*Aimez-Vous Brahms?* and *Un Certain Sourire* among them—in a career that included more than thirty novels, plays and cinema scripts.

"If none of her later work equaled the success of her debut, she always wrote with irony and elegance about passion and loss in the well-heeled milieu she knew. When the press concentrated less on her prose style than on the way her books reflected her lifestyle—the fast cars, the drink, men, gambling and drugs—she responded with typical wit that she did not think she could write convincingly about 'knitting, housekeeping and one's savings.' " —*Financial Times* (London), September 2004

The Book

"Sagan said that she wrote the book [*Bonjour Tristesse*] in two months, typing with two fingers. She met accusations of immorality with vigor and sold more than one million copies." —*Australian*, September 2004

"Asked how her daddy, a happily married Paris manufacturer, felt about the autobiographical air of *Bonjour*—a first-person, intimate chronicle of a young girl who lives cozily with her father and his sundry mistresses—Françoise gasped: 'Oh, poor Papa!' Chimed in her sister Suzanne, along on the trip: 'But no! Papa would be flattered!' " —*Time*, April 1955

"France's famed Roman Catholic novelist, François Mauriac, said the book was clearly written by the devil, and that did not harm its sales."
—*Time*, February 1955

"General de Gaulle was perplexed by the book, and struck by the author's air of social respectability." —*Guardian* (London), September 2004

"In a *New Yorker* article, John Updike applauded *Bonjour Tristesse* for 'its sparkling sea and secluding woods, its animal quickness, its academically efficient plot, its heroes and heroines given the perfection of Racine personae by the young author's innocent belief in glamour.' "
—*Washington Post*, September 2004

The End

"Sagan, who by all reports was extraordinarily generous in her heyday, died in Dickensian poverty, after years in miserable health and totally dependent on the charity of her friends. She owed large sums to the tax authorities. Her grand Normandy property had been seized, her race horses had long been sold, the sports cars with which she had been identified since her youth had gone. —*Guardian* (London), September 2004

Françoise Sagan: The *Paris Review* Interview, August 1956

FRANÇOISE SAGAN now lives in a small and modern ground-floor apartment of her own on the Rue de Grenelle, where she is busily writing a film script and some song lyrics as well as a new novel. But when she interviewed early last spring just before the publication of *Un Certain Sourire*, she lived across the city in her parents' apartment on the Boulevard Malesherbes in a neighborhood that is a stronghold of the well-to-do French bourgeoisie. She met the interviewers in the comfortably furnished living room, seated them in large chairs drawn up to a marble fireplace, and offered them scotch from a pint bottle which was unquestionably, somehow, her own contribution to the larder. Her manner is shy, but casual and friendly, and her gamine face crinkles easily into an attractive, rather secret smile. She wore a simple black sweater and gray skirt; if she is a vain girl the only indication of it was her high-heeled shoes, which were of elegantly worked light gray leather. She speaks in a high-pitched but quiet voice and she clearly does not enjoy being interviewed or asked to articulate in a formal way what are, to her, natural assumptions about her writing. She is sincere and helpful, but questions that are pompous or elaborate, or about personal life, or that might be interpreted as challenging her work, are liable to elicit only a simple "*oui*" or "*non*," or "*je ne sais pas—je ne sais pas du tout*"—and then an amused, disconcerting smile.

—*Blair Fuller & Robert B. Silvers, 1956*

INTERVIEWER: How did you come to start *Bonjour Tristesse* when you were eighteen? Did you expect it would be published?

FRANÇOISE SAGAN: I simply started it. I had a strong desire to write and some free time. I said to myself, This is the sort of enterprise very, very few girls of my age devote themselves to; I'll never be able to finish it. I wasn't thinking about "literature" and literary problems, but about myself and whether I had the necessary willpower.

INTERVIEWER: Did you let it drop and then take it up again?

FRANÇOISE SAGAN: No, I wanted passionately to finish it—I've never wanted anything so much. While I was writing I thought there might be a chance of its being published. Finally, when it was done, I thought it was hopeless. I was surprised by the book and by myself.

INTERVIEWER: Had you wanted to write for a long time before?

FRANÇOISE SAGAN: Yes, I had read a lot of stories. It seemed to me impossible not to want to write one. Instead of leaving for Chile with a band of gangsters, one stays in Paris and writes a novel. That seems to me the great adventure.

INTERVIEWER: How quickly did it go? Had you thought out the story in advance?

FRANÇOISE SAGAN: For *Bonjour Tristesse* all I started with was the idea of a character, the girl, but nothing really came of it until my pen was in hand. I have to start to write to have ideas. I wrote *Bonjour Tristesse* in two or three months, working two or three hours a day. *Un Certain Sourire* was different. I made a number of little notes and then thought about the book for two years. When I started in writing, again two hours a day, it went very fast. When you make a decision to write according to a set schedule and really stick to it, you find yourself writing very fast. At least I do.

INTERVIEWER: Do you spend much time revising the style?

FRANÇOISE SAGAN: Very little.

INTERVIEWER: Then the work on the two novels didn't take more than five or six months in all?

FRANÇOISE SAGAN: Yes, it's a good way to make a living. ►

Françoise Sagan: The *Paris Review* Interview, August 1956 ***(continued)***

INTERVIEWER: You say the important thing at the start is a character?

FRANÇOISE SAGAN: A character, or a few characters, and perhaps an idea for a few of the scenes up to the middle of the book, but it all changes in the writing. For me writing is a question of finding a certain rhythm. I compare it to the rhythms of jazz. Much of the time life is a sort of rhythmic progression of three characters. If one tells oneself that life is like that, one feels it less arbitrary.

INTERVIEWER: Do you draw on the people you know for your characters?

FRANÇOISE SAGAN: I've tried very hard and I've never found any resemblance between the people I know and the people in my novels. I don't search for exactitude in portraying people. I try to give to imaginary people a kind of veracity. It would bore me to death to put into my novels the people I know. It seems to me that there are two kinds of trickery: the "fronts" people assume before one another's eyes, and the "front" a writer puts on the face of reality.

INTERVIEWER: Then you think it is a form of cheating to take directly from reality?

FRANÇOISE SAGAN: Certainly. Art must take reality by surprise. It takes those moments which are for us merely a moment, plus a moment, plus another moment, and arbitrarily transforms them into a special series of moments held together by a major emotion. Art should not, it seems to me, pose the "real" as a preoccupation. Nothing is more unreal than a certain sensory truth—the true feeling of a character—that is all.

Of course the illusion of art is to make one believe that great literature is very close to life, but exactly the opposite is true. Life is amorphous, literature is formal.

INTERVIEWER: There are certain activities in life with highly developed forms, for instance, horse racing. Are the jockeys less real because of that?

FRANÇOISE SAGAN: People possessed by strong passions for their activities, as jockeys may seem to be, don't give me the impression of being very real. They often seem like characters in novels, but *without* novels, like *The Flying Dutchman*.

INTERVIEWER: Do your characters stay in your mind after the book is finished? What kind of judgments do you make about them?

FRANÇOISE SAGAN: When the book is finished I immediately lose interest in the characters. And I *never* make moral judgments. All I would say is that a person was droll, or gay, or above all, a bore. Making judgments for or against my characters bores me enormously; it doesn't interest me at all. The only morality for a novelist is the morality of his *esthétique*. I write the books, they come to an end, and that's all that concerns me.

INTERVIEWER: When you finished *Bonjour Tristesse* did it undergo much revising by an editor?

FRANÇOISE SAGAN: A number of general suggestions were made about the first book. For example, there were several versions of the ending and in one of them Anne didn't die. Finally it was decided that the book would be stronger in the version in which she did.

INTERVIEWER: Did you learn anything from the published criticism of the book?

FRANÇOISE SAGAN: When the articles were agreeable I read them through. I never learned anything at all from them but I was astonished by their imagination and fecundity. They saw intentions I never had.

INTERVIEWER: How do you feel about *Bonjour Tristesse*?

FRANÇOISE SAGAN: I like *Un Certain Sourire* better, because it was more difficult. But I find *Bonjour Tristesse* amusing because it recalls a certain stage of my life. And I wouldn't change a word. What's done is done.

INTERVIEWER: Why do you say *Un Certain Sourire* is a more difficult book? ▶

Françoise Sagan: The *Paris Review* Interview, August 1956
(continued)

FRANÇOISE SAGAN: I didn't hold the same trump cards in writing the second book: no seaside summer-vacation atmosphere, no intrigue naively mounting to a climax, none of the gay cynicism of Cécile. And then it was difficult simply because it was the second book.

INTERVIEWER: Did you find it difficult to switch from the first person of *Bonjour Tristesse* to the third-person narrative of *Un Certain Sourire*?

FRANÇOISE SAGAN: Yes, it is harder, more limiting and disciplining. But I wouldn't make as much of that difficulty as some writers apparently do.

INTERVIEWER: What French writers do you admire and feel are important to you?

FRANÇOISE SAGAN: Oh, I don't know. Certainly Stendhal and Proust. I love their mastery of the narrative, and in some ways I find myself in definite need of them. For example, after Proust there are certain things that simply cannot be done again. He marks off for you the boundaries of your talent. He shows you the possibilities that lie in the treatment of character.

INTERVIEWER: What strikes you particularly about Proust's characters?

FRANÇOISE SAGAN: Perhaps the things that one does not know about them as much as the things one knows. For me, that is literature in the very best sense: after all the long and slow analyses one is far from knowing all the thoughts and facts and sides of Swann, for example—and that is as it should be. One has no desire at all to ask "Who was Swann?" To know who Proust was is quite enough. I don't know if that's clear: I mean to say that Swann belongs completely to Proust and it is impossible to imagine a Balzacian Swann, while one might well imagine a Proustian Marsay.

INTERVIEWER: Is it possible that novels get written because the novelist imagines himself in the role of a novelist writing a novel?

FRANÇOISE SAGAN: No, one assumes the role of hero and then seeks out "the novelist" who can write his story.

INTERVIEWER: And one always finds the same novelist?

FRANÇOISE SAGAN: Essentially, yes. Very broadly, I think one writes and rewrites the same book. I lead a character from book to book, I continue along with the same ideas. Only the angle of vision, the method, the lighting, change. Speaking very, very roughly, it seems to me there are two kinds of novels—there is that much choice. There are those which simply tell a story and sacrifice a great deal to the telling—like the books of Benjamin Constant, which *Bonjour Tristesse* and *Un Certain Sourire* resemble in construction. And then there are those books which attempt to discuss and probe the characters and events in the book—*un roman où l'on discute*. The pitfalls of both are obvious: in the simple narrative it often seems that the important questions are passed over. In the longer classical novel the digressions can impair the effectiveness.

INTERVIEWER: Would you like to write *un roman où l'on discute*?

FRANÇOISE SAGAN: Yes, I would like to write—in fact I'm now planning—a novel with a larger cast of characters—there will be three heroines—and with characters more diffuse and elastic than Dominique and Cécile and the others in the first two books. The novel I would like to write is one in which the hero would be freed from the demands of the plot, freed from the novel itself and from the author.

INTERVIEWER: To what extent do you recognize your limits and maintain a check on your ambitions?

FRANÇOISE SAGAN: Well, that is a pretty disagreeable question, isn't it? I recognize limitations in the sense that I've read Tolstoy and Dostoyevsky and Shakespeare. That's the best answer, I think. Aside from that I don't think of limiting myself.

INTERVIEWER: You've very quickly made a lot of money. Has it changed your life? Do you make a distinction between writing novels for money and writing seriously, as some American and French writers do? ▸

Françoise Sagan: The *Paris Review* Interview, August 1956
(continued)

FRANÇOISE SAGAN: Of course the success of the books has changed my life somewhat because I have a lot of money to spend if I wish, but as far as my position in life is concerned, it hasn't changed much. Now I have a car but I've always eaten steaks. You know, to have a lot of money in one's pocket is nice, but that's all. The prospect of making more or less money would never affect the way I write—I write the books, and if money appears afterward, *tant mieux.*

Mlle. Sagan interrupted the interviewers to say that she had to leave to work on a radio program. She apologized and got up to go. It was difficult to believe, once she had stopped talking, that the slight, engaging girl had, with a single book, reached more readers than most novelists do in a lifetime. Rather, one would have thought her a schoolgirl rushing off to the Sorbonne as she called down the apartment hall to her mother, "Au revoir, maman. Je sors travailler mais je rentre de bonne heure."

The foregoing interview is reprinted by permission of Blair Fuller and Robert B. Silvers.

"Speeding"
An Essay by Françoise Sagan

THE PLANE TREES at the side of the road seem to lie flat; at night the neon lights of gas stations are lengthened and distorted; your tires no longer screech, but are suddenly muffled and quietly attentive; even your sorrows are swept away: however madly and hopelessly in love you may be, at 120 miles an hour you are less so. Your blood no longer congeals around your heart; your blood throbs to the extremities of your body; to your fingertips, your toes and your eyelids, now the fateful and tireless guardians of your own life. It's crazy how your body, your nerves and your senses hold you in the grip of life. For who has not thought that life was pointless without that other person, and put his foot down on an accelerator at once responsive and resistant? Who has not then felt his whole body tense, his right hand move to stroke the gears while his left hand grips the steering wheel, legs outstretched, deceptively relaxed, but ready for a violent jolt, ready to swerve and brake? And while taking all these precautions to remain alive, who has not thrilled to the awesome and fascinating silence of imminent death, at once a rebuttal and a provocation? Whoever has not thrilled to speed has not thrilled to life—or perhaps has never loved anyone.

First, there is, outside, this metal animal, to all eyes quietly sleeping, though you can wake it with a turn of a magic key. It coughs; you allow it to catch its breath, recover its voice and come to grips with another day, just as you would a friend who has woken too quickly. You gently propel this animal in the direction of the town and its streets, or the countryside and its ►

"However madly and hopelessly in love you may be, at 120 miles an hour you are less so."

lanes. Its engine gradually warms up, settling down to its own pace, slowly becoming excited by what it sees just as you do: fields or embankments, whichever, smooth surfaces to glide over and shoot along, bettering previous performance. You glance past cars to right and left, or, impatiently, mark time behind some debilitated road hog just in front of you. And then there's the same reflex: left foot down, wrist up a little, and with a slight jerk your car surges forward and overtakes the one in front, then settles down to a gently purring pace. This metal box flows through the arteries of the city and slips between its banks, emerging into squares, as if circulating in some vast vascular system it has no wish to block. Or this same metal box rolls through the countryside in the morning emerging from curtains of fog to rosy fields and shadowy borders, with the added danger of a steep incline now and again; the car stutters and again your left foot goes down and your right hand moves up and there is a joyous uphill surge, the small challenge of the climb causing the car to complain, but as soon as the road levels out it recovers its even rhythm. You are completely in control. The noises the car makes are subtly pleasing to the ear and to your body. There is no jolting, and you disdain to use the brakes. You are an eye above all else, the eye of the driver of this metal creature, an exquisite, highly strung creature that is useful but lethal—and what does that matter? You are an attentive, confident, mistrustful, busy, casual eye; motionless but quick, searching for someone else, making a desperate effort, not to find this other person now lost forever, but, on the contrary, to avoid any encounter.

At night the car shoots out of a bend into minefields, into fields strewn with the unforeseen, misleading lights and blinding yellow arcs across the sky; your headlights pick out what masquerade as wide roadways at the bottoms of ditches, and a host of other traps like where the ground falls away at the edge of your high beams; and there are all these unknown human beings you drive past, striking them as they connive to strike you with all the violence of the air between you forced out by your passing cars. All these unidentified drivers, all these enemies who dazzle you, leaving you dazed and disoriented on some asphalt strip beneath the furtive and deceptive moonlight. And sometimes you feel terribly drawn to the right, toward the trees that line the road, or to the left and the oncoming traffic—you want to escape somewhere, somehow, to avoid their raging headlights.

And there are those rest stops, all concrete, soda and small change, where highway adventurers take refuge, having escaped the domination of their own instinctive reflexes. And how quiet and peaceful it is there. It seems the black coffee you drank there could easily have been your last, the trailers on the road at Auxerre were so crazy, and you yourself could hardly see the road in front of you, what with the hailstorm and ice. Every one of the countless modest heroes of the highway is so used to brushes with death that it doesn't occur to him to make an issue of it. He just keeps going, driving along, eyes blinking in the headlights, his imagination working on what might happen. Is he going to overtake that car now? Do I have time to get by? His hands are ice-cold, sometimes his heart stops beating. You come across these cautious, silent heroes every night on the highway and at truck stops; they are in a hurry, tired, dogged, above all worried because it is still some sixty miles from Lyons to Valence, or Paris to Rouen, and after Mantes or Chalon there are only so many places you can stop, and so many places to tank up. So you take advantage of these stopovers and pull out of the game for five minutes. Still in one piece, safe in the shadow of the station billboard, you sit there watching the cars that were following you, or that you overtook in the past hour, drive past like kamikaze pilots. And there you take a deep breath, acting as if you will be in these temporary—so very temporary—refuges for good, refuges you will have to leave even if you become suddenly afraid of the black monsters to the rear and in front of you, and of their violent glaring beams that pierce the night and madden you. Then you take hold of yourself, or what's left of you and your machine; the engine moans and purrs and carries you off—you at the mercy of your engine, the engine at yours. And when you are back in your seat on your own plastic or leather cushion, with the smell of your own cigarettes, as your warm quick hand touches the cold wood or Bakelite of the steering wheel that has brought you this far and will, with luck, take you farther on your travels, then you know that a car is not just a means of transport but also an object of mythic proportions, possibly the instrument of your Destiny, capable of bring about your downfall or your salvation; it is Hippolytus's chariot, and not the ten thousandth replica off a production line.

Contrary to what one might think, the tempos of speed are not those of music. It is not the *allegro*, *vivace*, or *furioso* in a symphony which corresponds to 120 miles an hour, but the *andante*, the slow, majestic movement, a sort of plateau that you reach above a certain speed, when the car no longer protests, when there is no acceleration, just the opposite, in fact; the car and your body drift in harmony into a sort of alert and attentive state of giddiness, normally described as intoxicating. This ▶

sort of thing happens at night on a road in the middle of nowhere, and sometimes during the day in deserted places. When it happens the words "prohibited," "fasten seatbelts," "social security," "hospital," "death" no longer have any meaning, have been simply wiped out by a single word that men have used throughout the ages, a word that describes a silver racing car or a chestnut horse: the word "speed." The kind of speed you reach when something inside you outstrips something exterior to your body; that moment when the indomitable violence of a machine breaks loose or when an animal reverts to its wild state, and all your intelligence and sensibility and skill—and sensuality too—are barely able to control it; certainly your control is so tenuous there's still room for pleasure, and still room for the possibility such pleasure will prove fatal. Ours is a hateful age in which risk, the unpredictable, the illogical are constantly rejected, held up against numbers and deficits and calculations; it is a mean-spirited age that forbids people to kill themselves not because of the immeasurable value of their souls but because of the immediately computable price of their carcasses.

The truth of the matter is that a car—your car—endows you as its slave and master with the paradoxical sensation of being free at last, or returning to the maternal bosom, to an original state of solitude, far from alien eyes. Neither pedestrians, nor policemen, nor fellow motorists, nor the woman who might be waiting for him, nor all of life that waits for no man can separate the driver from his car, the only one of his possessions, after all, which allows him, for an hour a day, to rediscover in tangible form the solitude he was born to. And if the waves of traffic divide before the driver's car like the Red Sea before the Israelites; if red lights occur at greater intervals, more and more infrequently, until they disappear altogether; and if the road begins to shimmy and whisper in response to his foot on the accelerator; if the wind tears past his door like a hurricane; if each bend is a danger and a surprise, and each mile marks a small victory—why be surprised that imperturbable bureaucrats destined for brilliant careers within their companies should go and immolate themselves in glorious pirouettes of metal and gravel and blood, in final celebration of their terrestrial nature and ultimate defiance of what the future holds for them? These somersaults are described as accidents; loss of concentration, absent-mindedness are offered as explanations—everything except the most important reason, which is the exact opposite of these. It is the sudden unanticipated and irresistible fusion of body and soul, when a human being has an abrupt and fleeting insight into the nature of existence: Who on earth am I? I am myself, I am alive, this is what living means. I travel at fifty miles an hour through towns, seventy on main roads, eighty on highways, three hundred in my mind, though it feels like three in my skin—all in accordance with the highway code, the conventions of society and the laws of despair. What are these meaningless scales of numbers which have dogged me since childhood? Why should the speed of my life be dictated to me, when one life is all I have . . .

But now we digress from the idea of pleasure, of speed as pleasure, which, when all is said and done, is the best definition. And let me say it straight out, like Morand, like Proust, like Dumas: there is nothing imprecise, formless or shameful about this pleasure. It is a clearly defined, exultant and almost serene pleasure to drive too fast, exceeding the limitations of the car and the surface on which you are driving, exceeding the car's capacity to hold the road and perhaps even your own reflexes. And let me be clear that this is not a wager against oneself, nor an idiotic challenge to one's own skill; it is no showdown of self against self, or victory over some personal impediment. It is, rather, a lighthearted gamble between oneself and pure chance. When you go fast there is a moment when everything begins to float inside this metal vessel, when you reach the razor's edge, the crest of the wave, and you hope to come down on the right side, thanks not so much to your skill as to the direction of the current. A taste for speed has nothing to do with sport. Just as speed is tied with the idea of risk-taking and chance, so too is it tied to the joy of being alive, and therefore the vague death wish of which there is always a trace where there is *joie de vivre*. Well, that is everything that I believe to be true—speed is neither signal, nor proof, nor provocation, nor challenge; it is a surge of happiness.

"Speeding," translated by Christine Donougher, appeared in With Fondest Regards, *a collection of essays by Françoise Sagan (New York: E.P. Dutton, 1985).*

© 1984, Editions Gallimard, Paris

Don't miss the next book by your favorite author.

Sign up now for AuthorTracker by visiting

www.AuthorTracker.com.

Made in the USA
Middletown, DE
21 July 2020